SC
EAR

Earley, Tony

Here we are in
paradise

$19.45

DATE			
1-5-05			

HERE WE ARE IN PARADISE

HERE WE ARE IN PARADISE

Stories by
Tony Earley

LITTLE, BROWN AND COMPANY
BOSTON   NEW YORK   TORONTO   LONDON

First Edition

The characters and events in this book are fictitious.
Any similarity to real persons, living or dead, is coincidental
and not intended by the author.

Grateful acknowledgment is made to the following publications
in which some of these stories were first published:
New Stories from the South: "Charlotte"; *Best American Short Stories
1993:* "Charlotte"; *Harper's:* "Charlotte" and "The Prophet from Jupiter"; *TriQuarterly:* "My Father's Heart"; *Oxford Magazine:* "Here We
Are in Paradise"; *Mississippi Review:* "Story of Pictures"; *Witness:* "Aliceville" (under the title "The Simple Presence of Geese"). "Aliceville" was
also read on National Public Radio's "The Sound of Writing" under the
title "The Simple Presence of Geese."

Library of Congress Cataloging-in-Publication Data

Earley, Tony.
    Here we are in paradise : stories / by Tony Earley. — 1st ed.
        p.   cm.
    ISBN 0-316-19962-1
    1. City and town life — Southern States — Fiction.   I. Title.
PS3555.A685H47   1994
813'.54 — dc20   93-10789

10 9 8 7 6 5 4 3 2 1

RRD-VA

*Published simultaneously in Canada
by Little, Brown & Company (Canada) Limited*

Printed in the United States of America

For Reba and Charles;
for Clara Mae

He was still too young to know that the heart's
memory eliminates the bad and magnifies the good,
and that thanks to this artifice we manage
to endure the burden of the past.
— Gabriel García Márquez,
Love in the Time of Cholera

CONTENTS

HERE WE ARE
IN PARADISE

THE PROPHET
FROM JUPITER

MY HOUSE, the damkeeper's house, sits above the lake on Pierce-Arrow Point. The dam juts out of the end of the point and curves away across the cove into the ridge on the other side of the channel. On this side is the water, 115 feet deep at the base of the dam, and on the other side is air: the gorge, the river starting up again, rocks far down below, a vista. Seen from my windows, the dam looks like a bridge. There are houses on hundred-foot lots all the way around the lake, and too many real estate brokers. They all have jangling pockets full of keys, and four-wheel-drive station wagons with coffee cups sitting on the dashboards. The coffee cups are bigger at the bottom than they are at the top. Sometimes, at night, the real estate brokers pull up each other's signs and sling them into the lake.

A family on Tryon Bay has a Labrador retriever that swims in circles for hours, chasing ducks. Tourists stop on the bridge that crosses the bay and take the dog's picture. You can buy postcards in town with the dog on the front, swimming, swimming, the ducks always just out of reach. There is a red and white sign on the Tryon Bay Bridge that says NO JUMPING OR DIVING FROM BRIDGE, but teenage boys taunting each other and drunk on beer climb onto the rail and fling themselves off. I could drop the water level down a foot and a half any summer Saturday and paralyze all I wanted. Sometimes rednecks whoop and yell *Nigger!* and throw beer bottles at Junie Wilson, who walks up and down Highway 20 with a coat hanger around his neck. Junie drops a dollar bill into the water every time he crosses the bridge.

The Prophet from Jupiter brings his five young sons to the bridge to watch the Lab swim. The six of them stand in a line at the guardrail and clap and wave their arms and shout encouragement to the dog. The Prophet drives an ancient blue Lincoln that is big as a yacht. He says he drove it in another life, meaning Florida. Down in the water, the ducks let the dog get almost to them before they fly away. They fly maybe thirty, forty yards, that's all, and splash back down. The townies call the dog Shithead. You may not believe me, but I swear I have heard ducks laugh. Shithead, as he paddles around the bay, puffs like he is dying. This is where I live and this is what I think: a dam is an unnatural thing, like a diaphragm.

The most important part of my job is to maintain a constant pond level. But the lake rises all night, every night; the river never stops. This will worry you after a while. When I drive below town, coming back toward home, I'm afraid I'll meet the lake coming down through the gorge. When Lake Glen was built, it covered the old town of Uree with eighty-five feet of water. As the dam was raised higher and higher across the river, workmen cut the steeple off the Uree Baptist Church so it would not stick up through the water, but they did not tear down the houses. Fish swim in and out of the doors. Old Man Bill Burdette, who lived beside the church, left his 1916 chain-drive Reo truck parked beside his house when he moved away.

The diver who inspected the dam in 1961 told the Mayor that he saw a catfish as big as a man swimming by the floodgates. It is a local legend, the size of the catfish the diver saw. At night I fish for it, from the catwalk connecting the floodgates, using deep-sea tackle and cow guts for bait. It hangs in the water facing the dam, just above the lake's muddy bottom. Its tail moves slowly, and it listens to the faint sound of the river glittering on the other side of the concrete. The Prophet from Jupiter says, *When you pull your giant fish out of the water, it will speak true words.* When they tell history, people will remember me because of the fish, even if I don't catch it.

The Prophet from Jupiter's real name is Archie Simpson. He sold real estate, and made a fortune, in Jupiter, Florida, until nine years ago, when God told him — just as he closed a $4 million condominium deal in Port St. Lucie — that he was the one true prophet who would lead the Christians in the last days before the Rapture. The Prophet says his first words after God finished talking were, *Jesus Christ, you gotta be kidding.* He is not shy about telling the story, and does not seem crazy. He has a young wife who wears beaded Indian headbands and does not shave under her arms.

Old Man Bill Burdette's four sons hired divers and dragged their father's Reo truck out of the lake fifty years to the day after the water rose. It was almost buried in mud, and hadn't rusted at all. The Burdette boys spent six thousand dollars restoring the old Reo and then said to anyone who would listen, *I don't know why Daddy left it. It was just like new.* Bill Junior, the eldest son, drives it in the town parade every Fourth of July, the back loaded with waving grandchildren. The oldest ones look embarrassed.

Before I start fishing, I pour ripe blood from the bottom of my bait bucket into the water. I use treble hooks sharp as razors. A reel like a winch. Randy, the assistant damkeeper, is an orderly at the hospital in Hendersonville, and fishes with me after he gets off work. He does not believe the story about the fish as big as a man. I fish all night. Sometimes small catfish, ripping intestines from the treble hooks (they shake their heads like dogs, pulling), impale themselves and make a small noise like crying when I pull them out of the water. I hold them by the tail and hit their heads against the rail of the catwalk and toss them backward over the edge of the dam.

At dawn I open the small gate that lets water into the turbine house, throw the generator switches — there are four — and go to bed. The Town of Lake Glen makes a million dollars a year selling electricity. Everybody who works for the Town of Lake Glen has a town truck to drive. The trucks are traded for new ones every two years, and Lake Glen town employees use them like whores, driving at high speed through all the potholes they possibly can, because the trucks do not have to last. The Prophet from Jupiter makes miniature ladder-backed chairs that he sells wholesale to the gift shops on the highway. His young wife braids long bands of cowhide into bullwhips and attaches them to clean pine handles. With a hot tool she burns a small cross and the words LAKE GLEN, NORTH CAROLINA on the sides of the handles. She once said to me, *I know that what my husband says about God is true because every time we make love he fills me with the most incredible light.* The bullwhips she makes hang, moving in the draft from the cars on the highway, in front of the gift shops, and tourists stop and buy them by the dozen. It is inexplicable. In town, in front of the Rogue Mountain Restaurant, there is a plywood cutout of a cross-eyed bear wearing patched overalls. The bear holds up a red and white sign that says EAT. Once, during lunch in the Rogue Mountain Restaurant, the Prophet from Jupiter looked down into his bowl of vegetable soup and said, *You know, in the last days Christians won't be able to get corn.* LAKE GLEN, NORTH CAROLINA. The high-voltage wires leading away from the turbine house, you can actually hear them hum.

Sometime during the afternoon — cartoons are on television, the turbines have spun all day, in the Town Hall they are counting money, the skiers are sunburned in their shining boats, and the fishermen are drunk — the water level drops back down to full pond and the alarm goes off. I get out of bed and go down the narrow stairs to the turbine house and close the gate. The lake leans out over me. I feel better when I get back to the top of the stairs. All around Lake Glen it is brilliant summer: the town policemen park beside the beach and look out from under the brims of their Smokey the Bear hats at the college girls glistening in the sun. The night of the Fourth of July, the main channel of the lake fills up with boats, and seen from the dam, the running lights on the dark water glitter like stars. The fireworks draw lines on the sky like the ghosts of the veins in your eyes after you have stared into the sun.

People who should know better play jokes on Junie Wilson. If they tell him that hair spray will scare away ghosts, he carries a can with him everywhere he goes, like Mace, until the joke gets around and somebody tells him differently. If they tell him that ghosts live in ski-boat gas tanks, he will not walk by the marina for days or get within two hundred yards of a fast boat. The Prophet from Jupiter says that Junie has the gift of true sight. The Mayor gives Junie rides to keep him out of trouble.

This is what it's like to live on Lake Glen: in the spring, before the water is warm enough for the skiers to get on the lake, the sun shines all the way through you and you twist down inside yourself, like a seed, and think about growing. There are red and white signs on

the water side of the dam that say DANGER MAIN-
TAIN A DISTANCE OF 200 YARDS, but you can't read
them from that far away. In April, the wind blows down
out of the mountains and across the cove toward my
house, and the sun and the water smell like my wife's
hair. I don't know any other way to tell you about it.
Along the western shore, in the campgrounds beside the
highway, gas lanterns glow like ghosts against the
mountain. Boys and girls who will never see one another
again, and somehow know it, make desperate promises
and rub against each other in the laurel; they wade in
their underwear in the cold river. In the summer night
bullwhips pop like rifles.

Lake Glen was built between the mountains — Rogue
Mountain and Rumbling Caesar — in 1927 by the Lake
Glen Development Company. They built the dam, the
municipal building, and a hotel with two hundred
rooms before the stock market crashed. My wife's name
is Elisabeth. She lives, until I leave Lake Glen, with her
mother in Monte Sano, Alabama, and has nothing to
say to me. Twice a day the town gives guided pontoon-
boat tours of the lake. The boat stops two hundred
yards from the dam, and I can hear the guide over the
tinny loudspeaker explain how it would be dangerous
to get any closer. Two summers ago the town made a
deal with the family on Tryon Bay to keep Shithead
penned until the tour boat came to the bay at ten and
two. The ducks, however, proved to be undependable.

Shithead in his pen became despondent. Tourists pay two dollars a pop to take the tour. The problem was that the ducks swim on Tryon Bay every day, you just never know when. Elisabeth says that for years I had nothing to say to her, and that I shouldn't expect her to have much to say to me. I am ashamed to admit that this is true. There are hurricane-fence gates at each end of the dam, and only Randy and the Mayor and I have keys. When fishermen approach it in boats, I stand in the kitchen and ring the alarm bell until they leave. They shout at me perched on top of a cliff of water. This is something they do not consider.

The old people say that when Aunt Plutina Williams left her house for the last time before the lake was flooded, she closed her windows and shut and locked the doors. The Lake Glen Development Company planned, before Black Friday, to build four more two-hundred-room hotels and five eighteen-hole golf courses. Some of the streets in the town of Lake Glen still have the old development company names: Air Strip Road, Yacht Club Drive, H. L. Mencken Circle.

Elisabeth, before she left, taught the church pre-school class every other Sunday, and when she got home from church repeated for me, word for word, everything the kids said. One Easter she brought her class here for an Easter-egg hunt, and when she unlatched the gate on the front porch, they tumbled in their new clothes down the grassy slope toward the lake. Elisabeth followed me down to the turbine house once, and over the roar of the generators screamed into my ear, *Why won't you talk to me? What are you holding back?* The new police chief asked for a key to the hurricane-fence gates, but the Mayor refused to give him one.

The Lake Glen Hotel is sold and renovated about every five years, and banners are hung across the front of it on the days it reopens. A crowd gathers and drinks free Cokes. Old men sit and watch from the shade under the arches of the municipal building. A Florida Yankee makes a speech about the coming renaissance in Lake Glen. The Mayor cuts the ribbon and everybody claps. Most of the old streets are dead ends. The town of Lake Glen doesn't have an air strip or a yacht club: the hotel never stays open longer than a season. Most of the time, the signs of every real estate broker in town are lined up in front of it like stiff flags.

Elisabeth stood in the lake that Easter in a new yellow dress; the water was up over her calves. With one hand, she pulled her skirt up slightly from the waist. She held a glass jar in the other hand and looked into the water. The children squealed on the bank. Maybe then, watching Elisabeth, I believed for a minute in the risen Christ. This is what has happened: my wife, Elisabeth, is pregnant with the new police chief's child. Randy never mentions my misfortune, unless I mention it first. I am grooming him to be the new damkeeper. From the catwalk at night we see in the distance across the channel the lights of the town. There is no reason to come here and stay in a hotel with two hundred rooms. There is no reason to stay here at all.

Randy fishes for crappie with an ultralight rod that

is limber as a switch, and will some nights pull seventy-five, a hundred, out of the dark water, glittering, like nickels. He comes to the dam straight from work and fishes in his white orderly clothes. He smells disinfected and doesn't stay all night. This is what I have done: I took the passenger-side shoulder harness out of my Town of Lake Glen truck and bolted it with long screw anchors to the side of the dam, behind the catwalk. I buckle up when I fish. I don't want to be pulled into the water.

Randy is twenty years old and already has two children. He is not married. His girlfriend is tall and skinny and mean-looking. Randy says she fucks like a cat. The old people say that the morning of the day the water came up, they loaded Aunt Plutina Williams into the bed of Old Man Bill Burdette's new truck. Somebody asked Aunt Plutina why she closed her windows and locked her doors, and she said, *Why you never know, sometime I just might want to come back.* Junie Wilson has seen her. I am afraid that someday I will see her, too. Maintain a constant pond level. The last time I slept with Elisabeth, two hearts beat inside her.

Randy will go far in this town. He knows how to live here without making anyone mad, which is a considerable gift. Sometimes I can see Elisabeth bending her back into the new police chief. Randy says don't think about it. He is an ex-redneck who learned the value of cutting his hair and being nice to Floridians. He someday might be mayor. He brought his girlfriend to the town employee barbecue and swim party at the Mayor's glass house, and her nipples were stiff, like buttons. My shoulder harness is a good thing: sometimes late at night I doze, leaning forward against it, and dream of something huge, suspended in the water beneath me, its eyes yellow and open. At the party I saw Randy whisper something into his girlfriend's ear. She looked down at the front of her shirt and said out loud, *Well Jesus Christ, Randy. What Do You Want Me To Do About It?*

During the summers in the thirties the Lake Glen Hotel was a refuge for people who could not afford to summer in the Berkshires or the Catskills anymore. Down the road from the hotel, where the Community Center is now, there was a dance pavilion built on wooden pilings out over the bay. Elisabeth stood in the lake in a new yellow dress, holding a jar. The kids from the Sunday school squatted at the edge of the water and helped her look for tadpoles. The Mayor was diagnosed with testicular cancer in the spring, and waits to see if he had his operation in time. He owns a mile and a half of undeveloped shoreline. Real estate brokers lick their lips.

From my dam I have caught catfish that weighed eighteen, twenty-four, and thirty-one pounds: just babies. Randy said the thirty-one-pounder was big enough. He thinks I should stop. I think I scare him. I got my picture in the paper in Hendersonville, holding up the fish. My beard is long and significant; the catfish looks wise. I mailed a copy to Elisabeth in Monte Sano.

The new police chief drives up to the hurricane-fence gate after Randy goes home and shines his spotlight on me. I don't even unbuckle my harness anymore. The Mayor is not running for reelection. I will stay until inauguration day. I learned this from the old men in the hardware store: the new police chief will live with Elisabeth and their child in the damkeeper's house; Randy's girlfriend is pregnant again, and the house isn't big enough for three kids. The Town of Lake Glen police cars are four-wheel-drive station wagons with blue lights on the dashboards. It is hard to tell the cops here from the real estate brokers.

The dance-pavilion orchestra was made up of college boys from Chapel Hill, and black musicians who had lost their summer hotel jobs up north. The college boys and the black men played nightly for tips, in their shirtsleeves on the covered bandstand, tunes that had been popular during the twenties, and on the open wooden floor out over the water the refugees danced under paper lanterns and blazing mosquito torches. Bootleggers dressed in overalls and wide-brimmed hats drove their Model T's down out of the laurel and sold moonshine in the parking lot.

The new police chief came here from New York State and is greatly admired by the Florida Yankees for his courtesy and creased trousers. I try to hate him, but it is too much like hating myself for what I have done, for what I have left undone. I am the man who didn't miss his water. Florida Yankees have too much money and nothing to do. They bitch about the municipal government and run against each other for city council. They drive to Hendersonville wearing sweat suits and walk around and around the mall. Randy will not express a preference for city council candidates, not even to me. He will go far. His girlfriend will be the first lady of the town of Lake Glen.

The Mayor came here on summer break from Chapel Hill in 1931 and never went back. He played second trumpet in the Lake Glen orchestra. He took his trust fund and bought land all the way around the lake for eighteen cents on the dollar. He is the only rich man I can stand to be around. At the end of the night, the Mayor says — three, four o'clock in the morning — after the band had packed up their instruments and walked back to the hotel, the last of the dancers stood at the pavilion rail and looked out at the lake. Fog grew up out of the water. Frogs screeched in the cattails near the river channel, and there were cold places in the air. I can hear the new police chief's radio as he sits in his Jeep, outside the gates of the dam. The Mayor says that the last dancers would peel off their clothes and dive white and naked into the foggy lake. He says that when they laughed, he could hear it from the road as he walked away, or from his boat as it drifted between the mountains on the black lake, just before first light.

I hear laughter sometimes, when I am on the catwalk at night, or faint music, coming over the water, and it makes me think about ghosts, about those ruined dancers, looking out across the lake. Some nights I think that if I drove over to the Community Center and turned off my lights, I could see them dancing on the fog. Junie Wilson has taught me to believe in ghosts. The music I hear comes from a distance: I can never make out the tune. I remember that Elisabeth used to put her heels against the bed and raise herself up — she used to push her breasts together with her hands. *Ghosts is with us everywhere,* Junie Wilson says. Whenever I drop the lake down at the end of the season, the old, sawed-off pilings from the dance pavilion stick up out of the mud like the ribs of a sunken boat.

The old people say that the town of Uree held a square dance on the bank of the river the night before the water came up. They say that Jim Skipper, drunk on moonshine, shit in the middle of his kitchen floor and set his house on fire. The week before, the Lake Glen Development Company dug up the dead in the Uree Baptist Church graveyard and reburied them beside the new brick church on the ridge overlooking Buffalo Shoals. They even provided new coffins for the two Confederate soldiers who had been buried wrapped in canvas. The work crews stole their brass buttons. This is something that happened: Elisabeth and I tried to have a baby for seven years before we went to see a fertility specialist in Asheville.

The old people say that the whole town whooped and danced in circles in front of Jim Skipper's burning house, and that boys and girls desperate for each other sneaked off and humped urgently in the deserted buildings, that last night before the town began to sink. All the trees around the town of Uree had been cut. They lay tangled where they fell. The dead twisted and turned in their new holes, away from the sound of the river.

During the Second World War the government ran the Lake Glen Hotel as a retreat for Army Air Corps officers on leave from Europe. The Mayor says that the pilots — the ones who were not joined at the hotel by their wives — lay in still rows on the beach all day, sweating moonshine, and at night went either to the dance pavilion — where they tried to screw summer girls, and girls who walked in homemade dresses down out of the laurel — or to the whorehouse on the second floor of the Glen Haven Restaurant, a mile outside the city limits, where the whores were from Charleston, some of them exotic and Gullah, and the jukebox thumped with swing. The Mayor says that the Glen Haven during the war was like Havana before the revolution. The house specialty was fried catfish, and hush puppies made with beer. The Prophet from Jupiter and his young wife live with their five sons in the Glen Haven building because the rent is so cheap. There are ten rooms upstairs, five on each side of a narrow hall. One room, the Prophet says, always smells like catfish, even though they have scrubbed it. One Sunday morning in the early spring, the Prophet's son Zeke told Elisabeth that he dreamed Jesus came to his house and pulled a big bucket of water out of a well and everybody drank from it.

The fertility specialist, Dr. Suzanne Childress, said that I had lethargic sperm. *I knew it wasn't me,* Elisabeth said. *I knew it wasn't me.*

Dr. Suzanne Childress said, *Your sperm count is normal. They just do not swim well enough to reach and fertilize Elisabeth's ova.*

They say that Jim Skipper camped out under his wagon for three weeks beside the rising lake. He borrowed a boat from the Lake Glen Development Company and paddled around the sinking houses. He looked in the windows until they disappeared, and he banged on the tin roofs with his paddle. He collected all the trash that floated to the surface — bottles and porch planks and blue mason jars — and put it in his wagon and studied it at night by a fire. He said he did not know how to live anywhere else. They say that before Jim Skipper shot himself, he stood in his borrowed boat and pissed down Old Man Bill Burdette's chimney.

Elisabeth said, *You always thought it was me, didn't you?*

Dr. Suzanne Childress said, *I think that perhaps we can correct your problem with dietary supplements. Vitamins. Do you exercise?*

Elisabeth said, *I'm ovulating right now. I can tell.*

Dr. Suzanne Childress said, *I know.*

They closed the dance pavilion for good in 1944 when a moonshiner named Rudy Thomas, in a fight over a Glen Haven whore, stabbed a B-27 pilot from New York eleven times and pushed him into the lake.

Rudy Thomas died of tuberculosis in Central Prison in Raleigh in 1951. They say that Jim Skipper was a good man but one crazy son of a bitch.

Several nights a week during his second summer in town, the Mayor leaned a chambermaid named Lavonia over the windscreen of his 1928 Chris-Craft and screwed her until his legs got so weak that he almost fell out of the boat. Junie Wilson says that the boxes on the sides of telephone poles — if the ghosts have turned them on — make him so drunk that he is afraid he is going to fall into the lake. The coat hanger around Junie's neck protects him from evil spirits.

Sweet Lavonia, the Mayor says, *had the kind of body that a young man would paint on the side of his airplane before he flew off to fight in a war.*

The young Mayor took his clothes off as he drove his boat fast across the dark lake. Lavonia waited between two boulders on the shore near Uree Shoals. The Mayor cut the engine and drifted into the cove. Lavonia stepped out from between the rocks, pulled her skirt up around her waist, and waded out to the boat. The white Mayor glowed in the darkness and played gospel songs on his trumpet while she walked through the water. There wasn't a house or a light in sight. Lavonia told him every night while he squeezed her breasts, *You're putting the devil inside of me.* The boat turned in the water, and the Mayor owned everything he could see.

Randy in his orderly clothes, jigging for crappie, tells

me there is nothing wrong with me, that to make a woman pregnant you have to fuck her in a certain way, that's all. You have to put your seed where it will take.

Junie Wilson woke me up one morning yelling, *Open the gate, open the gate.* One of the town cops had told him that ghosts wouldn't walk across a dam, that walking across a dam while it made electricity was the way for a man to get rid of his ghosts once and for all. Junie sees three ghosts in his dreams: he sees a man standing in a boat, he sees a woman looking out the window of a house underwater, and he sees his mama wading out into the lake. This dream torments Junie most, because he doesn't know how to swim. He stands on the bank and yells for her to come back. We walked across the dam, the water up close beside Junie, the air falling away beside me. Junie said, *She better get out of that water if she knows what's good for her.* What my wife said is true: I never thought it was me. Elisabeth after we made love kept her legs squeezed tight together, even after she went to sleep. *Ghosts is keeping me awake,* Junie said. *I got to get rid of these ghosts so I can get me some sleep. Ghosts is crucifying me.* Out in the bay the new police chief watched from his boat. The siren whooped once.

Something's wrong with me, Elisabeth whispered. *I can't have a baby.*

I said, *I still love you. Shhh.*

Before we went to see Dr. Suzanne Childress, I liked to sit astride Elisabeth, hard and slick between her breasts. Lavonia tried to kill the baby inside her by drinking two quarts of moonshine that she bought in the pavilion parking lot from a bootlegger named Big Julie Cooper. Junie didn't speak until he was four. Ghosts began to chase him when he was twelve. The first time Lavonia saw Junie touching himself, she whipped him with a belt and told him that if he ever did that again, a white man would come with a big knife and cut it off. Elisabeth, when I was finished, wiped her chest and neck off with a towel.

Bugs fly like angels into the white light of the gas lantern and then spin and fall into the water. Randy jabs the air with his index finger: *It's special pussy, man, way back in the back. It burns like fire.* The Mayor gave Lavonia a little money every month until she died, three years ago. He does not give money to Junie because Junie drops dollar bills off the Tryon Bay Bridge. He does it so that the ghosts won't turn on their machines when he walks by telephone poles. The Mayor says, *Jesus Christ, if I gave that boy a million dollars, he'd throw every bit of it off that damn bridge.*

Randy says, *Man, women go crazy when you start hitting that baby spot. They'll scratch the hell out of you. You gotta time it right, that's all. You gotta let it go when you hit it.* He slaps the back of one hand into the other. *Bang. You gotta get the pussy they don't want you to have.*

Junie Wilson and I walked back and forth across the dam until the alarm went off and I had to close the gate and shut down the generators. I didn't tell Junie about the machines in the turbine house. The new police chief still watched from the bay. Elisabeth said over the phone from Monte Sano, *I know you won't believe it now, but all I ever wanted was for you to pay attention to me.* In a sterile men's room in the doctor's office, I put my hands against the wall and Elisabeth jerked me off into a glass bottle. The Mayor eats bananas to keep his weight up. Junie Wilson said that he did not feel any better, and I said that walking across the dam does not always work.

In August the air over the lake is so thick you can see it, and distances through the haze look impossible to cross. The mountains disappear before lunch, and even the skiers in their fast boats get discouraged. The water is smooth and gray, and the town of Lake Glen shimmers across the channel like the place it tried to be. At the beach, policemen sit in their station wagons with the air conditioners running. The college girls are tanned the color of good baseball gloves. Randy's girlfriend is starting to gain weight, and Randy fishes less; the crappie have all but stopped biting. When it is this hot, I have trouble sleeping, even during the day, and eat white ice cream straight out of the box with a fat spoon. The Prophet from Jupiter winks and says that in hot weather his wife smells like good earth, and that God has blessed him in more ways than one. The Prophet and his wife have made love in every room at the Glen Haven. In the hot summer, the ghosts keep their machines turned on all the time, and Junie Wilson staggers through town like a drunk. If there is one true thing I know to tell you, it is this: in North Carolina, even in the mountains, it takes more than a month of your life to live through August.

September is no cooler, but the sky begins to brighten, like a promise. Gradually it changes from white back to blue, and the town begins to pack itself up for leaving. The college girls go first, their tans already fading, and motor homes with bicycles strapped to their backs groan up out of the campgrounds to the shimmering highway. Boys and girls damp with sweat sneak away to say good-bye in the laurel and make promises one last time. Around the lake, family by family, summer people close up their houses and go back to where they came from in June. The Florida Yankees have mercifully decided among themselves who the new mayor will be — he is from Fort Lauderdale and is running unopposed — but the council candidates drive around town at night and tear down each other's campaign posters. My beard is down to the middle of my chest. Junie Wilson walks through town with his hands held up beside his face like blinders, to keep from seeing the bright faces stapled to the telephone poles. At night, the frogs hum one long, deep note, and one afternoon I slept in front of a fan and dreamed it was spring: Elisabeth waded in the lake and I sat on the porch and held a baby whose hair smelled like the sun. When I wake up now, my bathroom makes me sad because the mirror is so big. I dialed a 1-900 number for a date and charged it to the Town of Lake Glen. A woman named Betty said she wanted me to come in her mouth. In the closed-up summer houses, burglar alarms squeal in frequencies that only bats can hear, and the lights burn all night, turned on and off by automatic timers, but the rooms are empty and still.

In the fall, the wild ducks fly away after the summer people in great, glittering vees. Maples catch fire on the sides of the mountains around the lake, and weekend tourists drive up from Charlotte and Greenville to point at the leaves and buy pumpkins. The ducks skim low over the channel in front of my house, their wings whistling like blood, and then cross the dam, suddenly very high in the air. The Floridians burn leaves in their yards and inhale the smoke like Mentholatum. Randy said, *Man, I hope there ain't going to be any hard feelings,* and stopped coming to fish. Early one morning my line stiffened and moved through the water for twenty yards. When I set the hook, the stiff rod bent double against a great weight. And then it was gone. And that was it. The next night the new police chief sat outside the gate in his Jeep and played an easy-listening radio station over his loudspeaker. In the town of Uree, Aunt Plutina Williams sits and looks out the window of her house. The sun is never brighter than a distant lantern. Jim Skipper wanders in and out of the houses. A giant fish moves through the air like a zeppelin. The new police chief said over the loudspeaker, *Look, chief, I just want,* and then stopped talking and backed up and drove away.

In November 1928 the Lake Glen dam almost washed away. A flash flood, shot brown with mud, boiled down out of the mountains after a week of rain, and the damkeeper, new at the job, did not open the floodgates in time. The water rose and filled the lake bed like a bowl before it spilled over the top of the dam. Old Man Bill Burdette, who lived five miles away, drove down the mountain in his new truck to warn people downstream: the lake had turned itself back into a river and was cutting a channel through the earth around the side of the dam.

They say that the men of the Lake Glen Development Company construction crews hauled six heavy freight wagons of red roofing slate from the hotel site and threw it over the side of the gorge. Local men, when they heard, came down out of the laurel and worked in the rain filling sandbags and tossing them into the hole. But still the water ran muddy around the side of the dam and over the tops of the sandbags and the roofing. The workers, without waiting for orders, rolled the six empty wagons in on top of the pile. They say that they carried all of the furniture and both stoves out of the damkeeper's house and threw them in. They pushed three Model T Fords belonging to the company, as well as the superintendent's personal Pierce-Arrow, into the channel the river had cut around the side of the dam. But the water still snaked its way through the wreckage, downhill toward the riverbed.

This October, Town of Lake Glen workmen hung huge red and yellow banners shaped like leaves from wires stretched between the telephone poles. They built cider stands and arts and crafts booths and a small plywood stage in the parking lot in front of the Lake Glen

Hotel. The Chamber of Commerce hired a small carnival for the third Saturday in the month, called the whole thing ColorFest!, and promoted it on the Asheville TV station. Hundreds of tourists showed up, wearing bright sweaters even though it was warm. I saw townies look at me when they thought I wasn't looking, and their eyes said I wonder what he's going to do. My beard is a torrent of hair. A high school clogging team from Hendersonville stomped on the wooden stage. Old men sat and watched from underneath the arches of the municipal building. Little boys stood at the edge of the stage and looked up through the swirling white petticoats of the girl dancers. Shithead's owners walked him through the crowd on a leash. The Prophet from Jupiter and his wife sold miniature ladder-backed chairs and bullwhips from a booth, and gave away spiritual tracts about the coming Rapture. An old Cherokee, wearing a Sioux war bonnet, for two dollars a pop posed for pictures with tourist kids. Junie Wilson, crying for somebody to help him before the white man came to get him, showed his erection to three of Old Man Bill Burdette's great-granddaughters, who were sitting in the back of the 1916 Reo truck.

In 1928 the workers at the collapsing dam looked at each other in the rain. Everything seemed lost. The superintendent of the Lake Glen Development Company produced a Colt revolver and a box of cartridges. Big Julie Cooper took the superintendent's gun when nobody else would and one at a time shot twenty-four development company mules right between the eyes.

The workers threw the dead and dying mules in on top of the cars and the wagons and the red roofing slate and the furniture and the stoves, before the rain slacked and the water retreated back to the lake side of the dam. Then the superintendent threw his hat into the gorge and danced a jig and said, *Boys, you don't miss your water until your dam starts to go.* When the roads dried out, the development company brought in a steam shovel to cover the debris and the mules with dirt and rock blasted from the sides of the mountains, but not before the weather cleared and warmed and the mules swelled and rotted in the late-autumn sun. They say that you could smell the mules for miles — some of them even exploded — and that workmen putting the roof on the hotel, at the other end of the channel, wore kerchiefs dipped in camphor tied around their faces. They say that a black funnel cloud of buzzards and crows spun in the air over the gorge, and that you could see it from a long way away. At night bears came down off of Rumbling Caesar and ate the rotting mules. It is all covered by a thick growth of kudzu now, and every winter, after the vines die, I think of digging into the still-visible spine in the gorge beside the dam to see what I can find. Big Julie Cooper says, *By God, now let me tell you something, that son of a bitch liked to of went.*

When Old Man Bill Burdette's three great-granddaughters screamed, the new police chief twisted Junie Wilson's arm behind his back. Junie screamed, *Jesus, Jesus, Oh God, Please Don't Cut Me,* and tried to get away. The whole ColorFest! crowd, including the Indian chief, ran up close and silently watched while Junie and the new police chief spun around and around. *I'm not going to hurt you, Junie,* the new police chief said. Two other town cops showed up and held Junie down while the new police chief very efficiently handcuffed him and tied his legs together with three bullwhips that the Mayor brought from the Prophet from Jupiter's booth. The new police chief covered Junie's erection with a red ColorFest! banner shaped like a leaf. Junie's coat hanger was bent and twisted around his face. The new police chief pulled it off and handed it to the Mayor. Junie screamed for his mother over and over until his eyes rolled back in his head and his body began to jerk. Shithead howled. The high school clogging team from Hendersonville the whole time stomped and spun, wild-eyed, on the flimsy plywood stage.

The first Monday after Thanksgiving, I raised one of the floodgates halfway and lowered the lake eight feet. Randy will fill the lake back up the first Monday in February. It will be his job to maintain a constant pond level, to hold the water in the air, to try to imagine what the weather will be four days or two weeks from now. Every day I try to piss off the river side of the dam in a stream that will reach from me to the bottom of the gorge, but it is impossible to do. The water comes apart in the air. When the lake level is down, the exposed pilings of the boathouses are spindly like the legs of old men. Randy's girlfriend has started to show, and her breasts are heavy. The new police chief spends three days

in Monte Sano with my wife every other week. The
hotel is dark and for sale and locked up tight.

When the water is down and the mud between the
shore and the water dries out, the people who live here
year-round rake the leaves and trash from the lake bottom in front of their houses, and replace the rotten
boards on their docks and the rotten rungs on their
uncovered ladders. All around the lake, circular saws
squeal. The water over the town of Uree seems darker
somehow than the rest of the lake, and I've always
wanted to drop the lake down far enough to see what is
down there. At the end of that last night, when Jim Skipper's house had burned down to a glowing pile of ashes,
the people of the town of Uree sang, "Shall We Gather
at the River Where Bright Angel Feet Have Trod," and
then stood around, just looking at their houses and
barns and sheds, wishing they had done more, until the
sun came over the dam at the head of the gorge.

The Mayor stays mostly in his house now. His suc-
cessor has been elected. Randy wore a tie and met with
the mayor-elect to discuss ways to generate electricity
more efficiently. The Mayor keeps his thermostat set at
eighty-five and still cannot get warm. The word from the
state hospital in Morganton is that Junie Wilson has no
idea where he is or what has happened and screams
every time he sees a white doctor.

The lake began to freeze during a cold snap the week
before Christmas. There were circles of whiter ice over
the deeper water where part of the lake thawed in the

sun and then refroze again at night. The temperature dropped fast all day Christmas Eve, and the ice closed in and trapped a tame duck on Tryon Bay. Shithead, going out after the duck, broke through a soft spot in the ice and could not get back out.

Within fifteen minutes, most of the people who live in the town of Lake Glen were on the Tryon Bay Bridge, screaming, *Come On, Shithead, Come On, Boy, You Can Do It.* Nobody could remember who had a canoe, or think of how to rescue the dog. The Prophet from Jupiter, before anyone could stop him, ran across the frozen mud and slid headfirst like a baseball player out onto the ice. The duck frozen to the lake in the middle of the bay flailed its wings. I stood beside the new police chief on the bank and screamed to the Prophet, *Lie Still, Lie Still,* that we would find a way to save him.

The Prophet from Jupiter moved his lips and began to inch his way forward across the ice. It groaned under his weight. Cracks in the ice shot away from his body like frozen lightning. The Prophet kept going, an inch at a time, none of us breathing until he reached forward into the hole and grabbed Shithead by the collar and pulled him up onto the ice. It held. The dog quivered for a second and then skittered back toward shore, his belly low to the frozen lake.

We opened our mouths to cheer, but there was a crack like a gunshot, and the Prophet from Jupiter disappeared. He came up, once — he looked surprised more than anything else, his face deathly white, his mouth a black O — and then disappeared again and did not come back up. On the bridge the Prophet's five sons ran in place and screamed and held their arms toward the water. Randy's girlfriend kept her arms wrapped tight around the Prophet's wife, who shouted, *Oh Jesus, Oh Jesus,* and tried to jump off of the bridge. By the time we got boats onto the lake, and broke the ice with sledgehammers, and pulled grappling hooks on the ends of ropes through the dark water and hooked the Prophet and dragged him up, there was nothing even God could do. The duck frozen to the lake had beaten itself to death against the ice. The new police chief sat down on the bank and cried like a baby.

Elisabeth's water broke that night. The new police chief called the Mayor and left for Monte Sano, and the Mayor called me. I walked back and forth and back and forth across the dam until all the ghosts of Lake Glen buzzed in my ears like electricity: I saw the Prophet from Jupiter riding with Old Man Bill Burdette, down the streets of Uree in a 1916 Reo truck, toward the light in Aunt Plutina Williams's window; I saw catfish as big as men, with whiskers like bullwhips, lie down at the feet of the Prophet and speak in a thousand strange tongues; I saw dancers moving against each other in the air to music I had never heard; I saw Lavonia, naked and beautiful, bathing and healing Junie in a moonlit cove; I saw Elisabeth standing in the edge of the lake in the spring, nursing a child who smelled like the sun; I saw the new police chief in a boat watching over his family; I saw the Mayor on his knees praying in Gullah with Charleston whores; I saw Jim Skipper and Rudy Thomas and Big Julie Cooper driving a bleeding pilot beside the river in a wagon pulled by twenty-four mules; I saw the Prophet from Jupiter and his five young sons shoot out of the lake like Fourth of July rockets and shout with incredible light and tongues of fire, *Rise, Children of the Water, Rise, and Be Whole in the Kingdom of God.*

CHARLOTTE

THE PROFESSIONAL WRESTLERS are gone.
The professional wrestlers do not live here anymore.
Frannie Belk sold the Southeastern Wrestling Alliance to
Ted Turner for more money than you would think, and
the professional wrestlers sold their big houses on Lake
Norman and drove in their BMWs down I-85 to bigger
houses in Atlanta.

Gone are the Thundercats, Bill and Steve, and the
Hidden Pagans with their shiny red masks and secret
signs; gone is Paolo the Peruvian, who didn't speak
English very well but could momentarily hold off as
many as five angry men with his flying bare feet; gone
are Comrade Yerkov the Russian Assassin and his bald
nephew Boris, and the Sheik of the East and his Harem
of Three, and Hank Wilson Senior the Country Star
with his beloved guitar Leigh Ann; gone is Naoki Fujita,
who spit the mysterious Green Fire of the Orient into
the eyes of his opponents whenever the referee turned
his back; gone are the Superstud, the Mega Destroyer,

the Revenger, the Preacher, Ron Rowdy, Tom Tequila, the Gentle Giant, the Littlest Cowboy, Genghis Gandhi, and Bob the Sailor. Gone is Big Bill Boscoe, the ringside announcer, whose question "Tell me, Paolo, what happened in there?" brought forth the answer that all Charlotteans still know by heart — "Well, Beel, Hidden Pagan step on toe and hit head with chair and I no can fight no more"; gone are Rockin' Robbie Frazier, the Dreamer, the Viking, Captain Boogie Woogie, Harry the Hairdresser, and Yee-Hah O'Reilly the Cherokee Indian Chief. And gone is Lord Poetry, and all that he stood for, his arch-rival, Bob Noxious, and Darling Donnis — the Sweetheart of the SWA, the Prize Greater Than Any Belt — the girl who had to choose between the two of them, once and for all, during the Final Battle for Love.

Gone.

Now Charlotte has the NBA, and we tell ourselves we are a big deal. We dress in teal and purple and sit in traffic jams on the Billy Graham Parkway so that we can yell in the new coliseum for the Hornets, who are bad, bad, bad. They are hard to watch, and my seats are good. Whenever any of the Hornets come into the bar — and they do not come often — we stare up at them like they were exotic animals come to drink at our watering hole. They are too tall to talk to for very long, not enough like us, and they make me miss the old days. In the old days in Charlotte we did not take ourselves so seriously. Our heroes had platinum-blond hair and twenty-seven-inch biceps, but you knew who was good and who was evil, who was changing over to the other side and who was changing back. You knew that sooner or later the referee would look away just long enough for Bob Noxious to hit Lord Poetry with a folding chair. You knew that Lord Poetry would stare up from the canvas in stricken wonder, as if he had never once in his life seen a folding chair. (In the bar, we screamed at the television, "Turn around, ref, turn around!" "Look out, Lord Poetry, look out!") In the old days in Charlotte we did not have to decide whether the Hornets should trade Rex Chapman (they should not) or if J. R. Reid was big enough to play center in the NBA (he is, but only sometimes). In the old days our heroes were as superficial as we were — but we knew that — and their struggles were exaggerated versions of our own. Now we have the Hornets. They wear uniforms designed by Alexander Julian, and play hard and lose, and make us look into our souls. Now when we march disappointed out of the new coliseum to sit unmoving on the parkway, in cars we can't afford, we have to think about the things that are true: everyone in Charlotte is from somewhere else. Everyone in Charlotte tries to be something they are not. We spend more money than we make, but it doesn't help. We know that the Hornets will never make the playoffs, and that somehow it is our fault. Our lives are small and empty, and we thought they wouldn't be, once we moved to the city.

My girlfriend's name is Starla. She is beautiful and we wrestle about love. She does not like to say she loves me, even though we have been together four and a half years. She will not look at me when I say I love her, and if I wanted to, I could ball up the words and use them like a fist. Starla says she has strong lust for me, which should be enough; she says we have good chemistry, which is all anyone can hope for. Late in the night, after it is over, after we have grappled until the last drop of love is gone from our bodies, I say, "Starla, I can tell that you love me. You wouldn't be able to do it like that if you didn't love me." She sits up in bed, her head tilted forward so that her red hair almost covers her face, and picks the black hair that came from my chest off of her breasts and stomach. The skin across her chest is flushed red, patterned like a satellite photograph; it looks like a place I should know. She says, "I'm a grown woman and my body works. It has nothing to do with love." Like a lot of people in Charlotte, Starla has given up on love. In the old days Lord Poetry said to never give up, to always fight for love, but now he is gone to Atlanta with a big contract and a broken heart, and I have to do the best that I can. I hold on, even though Starla says she will not marry me. I have heard that Darling Donnis lives with Bob Noxious in a big condo in Buckhead. Starla wants to know why I can't be happy with what we have. We have good chemistry and apartments in Fourth Ward and German cars. She says it is enough to live with and more than anyone had where we came from. We can eat out whenever we want.

Starla breaks my heart.

She will say that she loves me only at the end of a great struggle, after she is too tired to fight anymore, and then she spits out the words, like a vomit, and calls me bastard or fucker or worse, and asks if the thing I have just done has made me happy. It does not make me happy, but it is what we do. It is the fight we fight. The next day we have dark circles under our eyes like the makeup only truly evil wrestlers wear, and we circle each other like animals in a cage that is too small, and what we feel then is nothing at all like love.

I manage a fern bar on Independence Boulevard near downtown, called P. J. O'Mulligan's Goodtimes Emporium. The regulars call the place PJ's. When you have just moved to Charlotte from McAdenville or Cherryville or Lawndale, and Independence is the only street you know, it makes you feel good to call somebody up and say, "Hey, let's meet after work at PJ's." It sounds like real life when you say it, and that is a sad thing. PJ's has fake Tiffany lampshades above the tables, with purple and teal hornets belligerent in the glass. It has fake antique Coca-Cola and Miller High Life and Pierce-Arrow automobile and Winchester Repeating Rifle signs screwed into the walls, and imitation bronze tiles glued to the ceiling. (The glue occasionally lets go and the tiles swoop down toward the tables, like bats.) The ferns are plastic because smoke and people dumping their drinks into the planters kill the real ones. The beer and mixed drinks are expensive, but the chairs and stools are cloth-upholstered and plush, and the ceiling lights in their smooth, round globes are low and pleasant enough, and the television set is huge and close to the bar and perpetually tuned to ESPN. Except when the Hornets are

on Channel 18, or wrestling is on TBS. In the old days
in Charlotte a lot of the professional wrestlers hung out
at PJ's. Sometimes Lord Poetry stopped by early in the
afternoon, after he was through working out, and tried
out a new poem he had found in one of his thick books.
The last time he came in, days before the Final Battle, I
asked him to tell me a poem I could say to Starla. In the
old days in Charlotte, you would not think twice about
hearing a giant man with long red hair recite a poem in
a bar, even in the middle of the afternoon. I turned the TV
down, and the two waitresses and the handful of hard-
cores who had sneaked away from their offices for a drink
saw what was happening and eased up close enough to
hear. Lord Poetry crossed his arms and stared straight
up, as if the poem he was searching for were written on
the ceiling, or somewhere on the other side, in a place we
couldn't see. His voice is higher and softer than you would
expect the voice of a man that size to be, and when he
nodded and finally began to speak, it was almost in a
whisper, and we all leaned in even closer. He said,

> *We sat grown quiet at the name of love;*
> *We saw the last embers of daylight die,*
> *And in the trembling blue-green of the sky*
> *A moon, worn as if it had been a shell*
> *Washed by time's waters as they rose and fell*
> *About the stars and broke in days and years.*
>
> *I had a thought for no one's but your ears:*
> *That you were beautiful, and that I strove*
> *To love you in the old high way of love;*

That it had all seemed happy, and yet we'd grown
As weary-hearted as that hollow moon.

P. J. O'Mulligan's was as quiet then as you will ever
hear it. All of Charlotte seemed still and listening
around us. Nobody moved until Lord Poetry finally
looked down and reached again for his beer and
said, "That's Yeats." Then we all moved back, suddenly
conscious of his great size, and our closeness to it, and
nodded and agreed that it was a real good poem, one of
the best we had ever heard him say. Later I had him
repeat it for me, line for line, and I wrote it down on a
cocktail napkin. Sometimes, late at night, after Starla
and I have fought, and I have made her say I love you
like uncle, even as I can see in her eyes how much she
hates me for it, I think about reading the poem to her,
but some things are just too true to ever say out loud.

In PJ's we watch wrestling still, even though we can
no longer claim it as our own. We sit around the big
screen without cheering, and stare at the wrestlers like
they are favorite relatives we haven't seen in years. We
say things like "Boy, the Viking has really put on weight
since he moved down there" or "When did Rockin'
Robbie Frazier cut his hair like that?" We put on brave
faces when we talk about Rockin' Robbie, who was
probably Charlotte's most popular wrestler, and try not
to dwell on the fact that he is gone away from us for
good. In the old days he dragged his stunned and half-
senseless opponents to the center of the ring and climbed
onto the top rope, and after the crowd counted down

from five (*Four! Three! Two! One!*) he would launch himself into the air, his arms and legs spread like wings, his blond hair streaming out behind him like a banner, and fly ten–fifteen feet, easy, and from an unimaginable height drop with a crash like an explosion directly onto his opponent's head. He called it the Rockin' Robbie B-52. ("I'll tell you one thing, Big Bill. Come next Saturday night in the Charlotte Coliseum I'm gonna B-52 the Sheik of the East like he ain't never been B-52ed before.") And after Rockin' Robbie's B-52 had landed, while his opponent flopped around on the canvas like a big fish, waiting only to be mounted and pinned, Rockin' Robbie leapt up and stood over him, his body slick with righteous sweat, his face a picture of joy. He held his hands high in the air, his fingers spread wide, his pelvis thrusting uncontrollably back and forth in the electric joy of the moment, and he tossed his head back and howled like a dog, his red lips aimed at the sky. Those were glorious days. Whenever Rockin' Robbie walked into PJ's, everybody in the place raised their glass and pointed their nose at the fake bronze of the ceiling and bayed at the stars we knew spun, only for us, in the high, moony night above Charlotte. Nothing like that happens here anymore. Frannie Belk gathered up all the good and evil in our city and sold it four hours south. These days the illusions we have left are the small ones of our own making, and they have in the vacuum the wrestlers left behind become too easy to see through; we now have to live with ourselves.

*   *   *

About once a week some guy who's just moved to
Charlotte from Kings Mountain or Chester or Gaffney
comes up to me where I sit at the bar, on my stool by
the waitress station, and says, "Hey, man, are you P. J.
O'Mulligan?" They are never kidding, and whenever it
happens I don't know what to say. I wish I could tell
them whatever it is they need in their hearts to hear, but
P. J. O'Mulligan is fourteen lawyers from Richmond
with investment capital. What do you say? New people
come to Charlotte from the small towns every day,
searching for lives that are bigger than the ones they
have known, but what they must settle for, once they
get here, are much smaller hopes: that maybe this year
the Hornets might really have a shot at the Celtics, if
Rex Chapman has a good game; that maybe there really
is somebody named P. J. O'Mulligan, and that maybe
that guy at the bar is him. Now that the wrestlers are
gone, I wonder about these things. How do you tell
somebody how to find what they're looking for when
ten years ago you came from the same place, and have
yet to find it yourself? How do you tell somebody from
Polkville or Aliceville or Cliffside, who just saw downtown after sunset for the first time, not to let the beauty
of the skyline fool them? Charlotte is a place where a
crooked TV preacher can steal money and grow like a
sore until he collapses from the weight of his own evil
by simply promising hope. So don't stare at the NCNB
Tower against the dark blue of the sky; keep your eyes
on the road. Don't think that Independence Boulevard
is anything more than a street. Most of my waitresses

are college girls from UNCC and CPCC, and I can see
the hope shining in their faces even as they fill out appli-
cations. They look good in their official P. J. O'Mulligan's khaki shorts and white sneakers and green aprons
and starched, preppy blouses, but they are still mill-
town girls through and through, come to the city to find
the answers to their prayers. How do you tell them
Charlotte isn't a good place to look? Charlotte is a place
where a crooked TV preacher can pray that his flock will
send him money so that he can build a giant water
slide — and they will. I prefer to hire waitresses from
Davidson or Queens College, because when they are
through with school they will live lives the rest of us can
only imagine, but they are easily disillusioned and hard
to keep for very long.

PJ's still draws a wrestling crowd. They are mostly good-
looking and wear lots of jewelry. The girls do aerobics
like religion and have big, curly hair, stiff with mousse.
They wear short, tight dresses — usually black — and
dangling earrings and spiked heels and lipstick with little sparkles in it, like stars, that you're not even sure you
can see. (You catch yourself staring at their mouths
when they talk, waiting for their lips to catch the light.)
The guys dye their hair blond and wear it spiked on top,
long and permed in back, and shaved over the ears.
They lift weights and take steroids. When they have
enough money they get coked up. They wear stone-
washed jeans and open shirts and gold chains thick as

ropes and cowboy boots made from python skin, which
is how professional wrestlers dress when they relax.
Sometimes you will see a group of guys in a circle, with
their jeans pulled up over their calves, arguing about
whose boots were made from the biggest snake. The
girls have long, red fingernails and work mostly in the
tall offices downtown. Most of the guys work out-
doors — construction usually, there still is a lot of that,
even now — or in the bodybuilding gyms, or the industrial parks along I-85. Both sexes are darkly and arti-
ficially tanned, even in the winter, and get drunk on
shooters and look vainly in PJ's for love.

Around midnight on Friday and Saturday, before
everyone clears out to go dancing at The Connection or
Plum Crazy's, where the night's hopes become final
choices, PJ's gets packed. The waitresses have to move
sideways through the crowd with their trays held over
their heads. Everybody shouts to be heard over each
other and over the music — P. J. O'Mulligan's official
contemporary jazz, piped in from Richmond — and if
you close your eyes and listen carefully you can hear in
the voices the one story they are trying not to tell: how
everyone in Charlotte grew up in a white house in a row
of white houses on the side of a hill in Lowell or Kan-
napolis or Spindale, and how they had to be quiet at
home because their daddies worked third shift, how a
black oil heater squatted like a gargoyle in the middle
of their living room floor, and how the whole time they
were growing up the one thing they always wanted to

do was leave. I get lonesome sometimes, in the buzzing middle of the weekend, when I listen to the voices and think about the shortness of the distance all of us managed to travel as we tried to get away, and how when we got to Charlotte the only people we found waiting for us were the ones we had left. Our parents go to tractor pulls and watch *Hee-Haw*. My father eats squirrel brains. We tell ourselves that we are different now, because we live in Charlotte, but deep down know that we are only making do.

The last great professional wrestling card Frannie Belk put together — before she signed Ted Turner's big check and with a diamond-studded wave of her hand sent the wrestlers away from Charlotte for good — was Armageddon V, The Last Explosion, which took place in the new coliseum three nights after the Hornets played and lost their first NBA game. ("Ohhhhhh," Big Bill Boscoe said in the promotional TV ad, his big voice quavering with emotion, "Ladies and Gentlemen and Wrestling Fans of All Ages, See an Unprecedented Galaxy of SWA Wrestling Stars Collide and Explode in the Charlotte Coliseum . . .") And for a while that night — even though we knew the wrestlers were moving to Atlanta — the world still seemed young and full of hope, and we were young in it, and life in Charlotte seemed close to the way we had always imagined it should be: Paolo the Peruvian jerked his bare foot out from under the big, black boot of Comrade Yerkov, and then kicked the shit out of him in a flying frenzy of

South American feet; Rockin' Robbie Frazier squirted a water pistol into Naoki Fujita's mouth, before Fujita could ignite the mysterious Green Fire of the Orient, and then launched a B-52 from such a great height that even the most jaded wrestling fans gasped with wonder (and if that wasn't enough, he later ran from the locker room in his street clothes, his hair still wet from his shower, his shirt tail out and flapping, and in a blond fury B-52ed not one, but both of the Hidden Pagans, who had used a folding chair to gain an unfair advantage over the Thundercats, Bill and Steve). And we saw the Littlest Cowboy and Chief Yee-Hah O'Reilly, their wrists bound together with an eight-foot leather thong, battle nobly in an Apache Death Match, until neither man was able to stand and the referee called it a draw and cut them loose with a long and crooked dagger belonging to the Sheik of the East; Hank Wilson Senior the Country Star whacked Captain Boogie Woogie over the head with his beloved guitar Leigh Ann, and earned a thoroughly satisfying disqualification and a long and heartfelt standing O; one of the Harem of Three slipped the Sheik of the East a handful of Arabian sand, which he threw into the eyes of Bob the Sailor to save himself from the Sailor's Killer Clam hold — from which no bad guy ever escaped, once it was locked — but the referee saw the Sheik do it (the rarest of wrestling miracles) and awarded the match to the Sailor; and in the prelude to the main event, like the thunder before a storm, the Brothers Clean — the Superstud, the Viking, and the Gentle Giant — outlasted the Three Evils — Genghis

Gandhi, Ron Rowdy, and Tom Tequila — in a six-man Texas Chain-Link Massacre match in which a ten-foot wire fence was lowered around the ring, and bald Boris Yerkov and Harry the Hairdresser patrolled outside, eyeing each other suspiciously, armed with bullwhips and folding chairs, to make sure that no one climbed out and no one climbed in.

Now, looking back, it seems prophetic somehow that Starla and I lined up on opposite sides during the Final Battle for Love. ("Sex is the biggest deal people have," Starla says. "You think about what you really want from me, what really matters, the next time you ask for a piece.") In the Final Battle, Starla wanted Bob Noxious, with his dark chemistry, to win Darling Donnis away from Lord Poetry once and for all. He had twice come close. I wanted Lord Poetry to strike a lasting blow for love. Starla said it would never happen, and she was right. Late in the night, after it is over, after Starla has pinned my shoulders flat against the bed and held them there, after we are able to talk, I say, "Starla, you have to admit that you were making love to me. I could tell." She runs to the bathroom, her legs stiff and close together, to get rid of part of me. "Cave men made up love," she calls out from behind the door. "After they invented laws, they had to stop killing each other, so they told their women they loved them to keep them from screwing other men. That's what love is."

Bob Noxious was Charlotte's most feared and evil wrestler, and on the night of the Final Battle, we knew

that he did not want Darling Donnis because he loved
her. Bob Noxious was scary: he had a cobalt-blue,
spiked mohawk, and if on his way to the ring a fan spat
on him, he always spat back. He had a neck like a bull,
and a fifty-six-inch chest, and he could twitch his pectoral muscles so fast that his nipples jerked up and down
like pistons. Lord Poetry was almost as big as Bob Noxious, and scary in different ways. His curly red hair was
longer than Starla's, and he wrestled in paisley tights —
pinks and magentas and lavenders — he had specially
made in England. He read a poem to Darling Donnis
before and after every match while the crowd yelled for
him to stop. (Charlotte did not know which it hated
more: Bob Noxious with his huge and savage evil, or
the prancing Lord Poetry with his paisley tights and fat
book of poems.) Darling Donnis was the picture of
innocence (and danger, if you are a man) and hung
on every word Lord Poetry said. She was blond, and
wore a low-cut, lacy white dress (but never a slip), and
covered her mouth with her hands whenever Lord
Poetry was in trouble, her moist, green eyes wide with
concern.

Darling Donnis's dilemma was this: she was in love
with Lord Poetry, but she was mesmerized by Bob Noxious's animal power. The last two times Bob Noxious
and Lord Poetry fought, before the Final Battle, Bob
Noxious had beaten Lord Poetry with his fists until Lord
Poetry couldn't stand, and then he turned to Darling
Donnis and put his hands on his hips and threw his

shoulders back, revealing enough muscles to make several lesser men. Darling Donnis's legs visibly wobbled, and she steadied herself against the ring apron, but she did not look away. While the crowd screamed for Bob Noxious to "Shake 'em! Shake 'em! Let 'em go!" he began to twitch his pectorals up and down, first just one at a time, just once or twice — teasing Darling Donnis — then the other, then in rhythm, faster and faster. It was something you had to look at, even if you didn't want to, a force of nature, and at both matches Darling Donnis was transfixed. She couldn't look away from Bob Noxious's chest, and would have gone to him (even though she held her hands over her mouth, and shook her head no, the pull was too strong) had it not been for Rockin' Robbie Frazier. At both matches before the Final Battle, Rockin' Robbie ran out of the locker room in his street clothes and tossed the prostrate Lord Poetry the book of poems that Darling Donnis had carelessly dropped on the apron of the ring. Then he climbed through the ropes and held off the enraged and bellowing Bob Noxious long enough for Lord Poetry to crawl out of danger and read Darling Donnis one of her favorite sonnets, which calmed her. But the night of the Final Battle, all of Charlotte knew that something had to give. We did not think that even Rockin' Robbie could save Darling Donnis from Bob Noxious three times. Bob Noxious's pull was too strong. This time Lord Poetry had to do it himself.

*   *   *

They cleared away the cage from the Texas Chain-Link Massacre, and the houselights went down slowly until only the ring was lit. The white canvas was so bright that it hurt your eyes to look at it. Blue spotlights blinked open in the high darkness beneath the roof of the coliseum, and quick circles of light skimmed across the surface of the crowd, showing in an instant a hundred–two hundred expectant faces. The crowd could feel the big thing coming up on them, like animals before an earthquake. Rednecks in the high, cheap seats stomped their feet and hooted like owls. Starla twisted in her seat and stuck two fingers into her mouth and cut loose with a shrill whistle. "Ohhhhh Ladies and Gentlemen and Wrestling Fans," Big Bill Boscoe said from everywhere in the darkness, like the very voice of God, "I Hope You Are Ready to Hold On to Your Seats" — and in their excitement 23,000 people screamed *Yeah!* — "Because the Earth Is Going to Shake and the Ground Is Going to Split Open" — *YEAH!*, louder now — "and Hellfire Will Shoot Out of the Primordial Darkness in a Holocaust of Pure Wrestling Fury" — they punched at the air with their fists, and roared, like beasts, the blackness they hid in their hearts, *YEAHHHHHHH!* "Ohhhhhh," Big Bill Boscoe said when they quieted down, his voice trailing off into a whisper filled with fear (he was afraid to unleash the thing that waited in the dark for the sound of his words, and they screamed in rage at his weakness, *YEAHHHHHHHH!*) "Ohhhhhh, Charlotte, Ohhhhhhh, Wrestling Fans and Ladies and Gentlemen, I

Hope, I Pray, That You Have Made Ready" —
YEAHHHHHHH! — "For . . . The FINAL . . . BAT-
TLE . . . FOR . . . LOOOOOOOOOVE!"

At the end of regulation time (nothing really important
ever happens in professional wrestling until the borrowed time after the final bell has rung) Bob Noxious
and Lord Poetry stood in the center of the ring, their
hands locked around each other's thick throat. Because
chokeholds are illegal in SWA professional wrestling, the
referee had ordered them to let go and, when they
refused, began to count them out for a double disqualification. Bob Noxious and Lord Poetry let go only long
enough to grab the referee, each by an arm, and throw
him out of the ring, where he lay prostrate on the floor.
Lord Poetry and Bob Noxious again locked onto each
other's throat. There was no one there to stop them, and
we felt our stomachs falling away into darkness, into the
chaos. Veins bulged like ropes beneath the skin of their
arms. Their faces were contorted with hatred, and
turned from pink to red to scarlet. Starla jumped up and
down beside me and shouted, "*KILL* Lord Poetry!
KILL Lord Poetry!"

Darling Donnis ran around and around the ring, beg-
ging for someone, anyone, to make them stop. At the
announcer's table, Big Bill Boscoe raised his hands in
helplessness. Sure he wanted to help, but he was only
Big Bill Boscoe, a voice. What could he do? Darling
Donnis rushed away. She circled the ring twice more
until she found Rockin' Robbie Frazier keeping his vigil

from the shadows near the entrance to the locker room. She dragged him into the light near the ring. She pointed wildly at Lord Poetry and Bob Noxious. Both men had started to shake, as if cold. Bob Noxious's eyes rolled back in his head, but he didn't let go. Lord Poetry stumbled, but reached back with a leg and regained his balance. Darling Donnis shouted at Rockin' Robbie. She pointed again. She pulled her hair. She doubled her hands under her chin, pleading. "*CHOKE* him!" Starla screamed. "*CHOKE* him!" She looked sideways at me. "*HURRY!*" Darling Donnis got down on her knees in front of Rockin' Robbie and wrapped her arms around his waist. Rockin' Robbie stroked her hair but stared into the distance and shook his head no. Not this time. This was what it had come to. This was a fair fight between men, and none of his business. He walked back into the darkness.

Darling Donnis was on her own now. She ran to the ring and stood at the apron and screamed for Bob Noxious and Lord Poetry to stop it. The sound of her words was lost in the roar that came from out of our hearts, but we could feel them. She pounded on the canvas, but they didn't listen. They kept choking each other, their fingers a deathly white. Darling Donnis crawled beneath the bottom rope and into the ring. "*NO!*" Starla yelled, striking the air with her fists. "Let him *DIE*. Let him *DIE!*" Darling Donnis took a step toward the two men and reached out with her hands, but stopped, unsure of what to do. She wrapped her arms around herself and rocked back and forth. She grabbed her hair and started to scream. She screamed as if the earth really had opened up, and hellfire had shot up all around her — and that it had been her fault. She screamed until her eyelids fluttered closed, and she dropped into a blond and white heap on the mat, and lay there without moving.

When Darling Donnis stopped screaming, it was as if the spell that had held Bob Noxious and Lord Poetry at each other's throat was suddenly broken. They let go at the same time. Lord Poetry dropped heavily to his elbows and knees, facing away from Darling Donnis. Bob Noxious staggered backward into the corner, where he leaned against the turnbuckles. He held on to the top rope with one hand, and with the other rubbed his throat. "Go *GET* her!" Starla screamed at Bob Noxious. "Go *GET* her!" For a long time nobody in the ring moved, and in the vast, enclosed darkness surrounding the ring, starting up high and then spreading throughout the building, 23,000 people began to stomp their feet. Tiny points of fire, hundreds of them, sparked in the darkness. But still Bob Noxious and Lord Poetry and Darling Donnis did not move. The crowd stomped louder and louder (*BOOM! BOOM! BOOM! BOOM!*) until finally Darling Donnis weakly raised her head, and pushed her hair back from her eyes. We caught our breath and looked to see where she looked. It was at Bob Noxious. Bob Noxious glanced suddenly up, his dark power returning. He took his hand off of his throat and put it on the top rope and pushed himself up higher. Darling Donnis raised herself onto her hands and knees and peeked quickly at Lord Poetry, who still hadn't moved, and then looked back to Bob Noxious. "*DO* it, Darling Donnis!" Starla screamed. "Just *DO* it!" Bob Noxious pushed off against the ropes and took an unsteady step forward. He inhaled deeply and stood up straight. Darling Donnis's eyes never left him. Bob Noxious put his hands on his hips, and with a monumental effort threw his great shoulders all the way back. *No,* we saw Darling Donnis whisper. *No.* High up in the seats beside me, Starla screamed, "*YES!*"

Bob Noxious's left nipple twitched once. Twitch. Then again. Then the right. The beginning of the end. Darling Donnis slid a hand almost imperceptibly toward him across the canvas. But then, just when it all seemed lost, Rockin' Robbie Frazier ran from out of the shadows to the edge of the ring. He carried a thick book in one hand and a cordless microphone in the other. He leaned under the bottom rope and began to shout at Lord Poetry, their faces almost touching. (*Lord Poetry! Lord Poetry!*) Lord Poetry finally looked up at Rockin' Robbie, and then slowly turned to look at Bob Noxious, whose pectoral muscles had begun to twitch regularly, left-right, left-right, like heartbeats. Darling Donnis raised a knee from the canvas and began to stalk Bob Noxious. Rockin' Robbie reached in through the ropes and helped Lord Poetry to his knees. He gave the book and the microphone to Lord Poetry. Lord Poetry turned around, still kneeling, until he faced Darling Donnis. She didn't even look at him. Five feet to Lord Poetry's right, Bob Noxious's huge chest was alive, pumping. A train picking up speed. Lord Poetry opened the book and turned to a page and shook his head. No, that one's not right. He turned farther back into the book and shook his head again. What is the one thing you can say to save the world you live in? How do you find the words? Darling Donnis licked her red lips. Rockin' Robbie began shouting and flashing his fingers in numbers at Lord Poetry. Ten-Eight. Ten-Eight. Lord Poetry looked over his shoulder at Rockin' Robbie, and his eyebrows moved up in a question: Eighteen? *Yes,* screamed Rockin' Robbie. *Eighteen.* Ten-eight. "Ladies and Gentlemen," Big Bill Boscoe's huge voice said, filled now with hope, "I think it's going to be Shakespeare's Sonnet Number Eighteen!" and a great shout of *NOOOOO!* rose up in the darkness like a wind.

Lord Poetry flipped through the book, and studied a page, and reached out and touched it, as if it were in Braille. He looked quickly at Darling Donnis, flat on her belly now, slithering across the ring toward Bob Noxious. Lord Poetry said into the microphone, "Shall I compare thee to a summer's day?" Starla kicked the seat in front of her and screamed, *"NO!* Don't Do It! Don't Do It! He's After Your *Soul!* He's After Your *Soul!"* Lord Poetry glanced up again and said, "Thou art more lovely and more temperate," and then faster, more urgently, "Rough winds do shake the darling buds of May," but Darling Donnis crawled on, underneath the force of his words, to within a foot of Bob Noxious. Bob Noxious's eyes were closed in concentration and pain, but still his pectorals pumped faster. Lord Poetry opened his mouth to speak again, but then looked one last time at Darling Donnis and buried his face in the book and slumped to the mat. Rockin' Robbie pulled on the ropes like they were the bars of a cage and yelled in rage, his face pointed upward, but he did not climb into the ring. He could not stop what was happening. *Please,* we saw Darling Donnis say to Bob Noxious. *Please.* The panicked voice of Big Bill Boscoe boomed out like thunder: "Darling Donnis! Darling Donnis! And summer's lease hath all too short a date! Sometime too hot the eye of heaven shines! And often is his gold complexion dimm'd!" But it was too late: Bob Noxious reached down and lifted Darling Donnis up by the shoulders. She looked him straight in the eye and reached out with both hands and touched his broad, electric chest. Her eyes rolled back in her head. Starla dropped heavily down into her seat, and breathed deeply, twice. She looked up at me and smiled. "There," she said, as if it were late in the night, as if it were over. "There."

HERE WE ARE
IN PARADISE

BECAUSE he did not know what else to do, Vernon
Jackson bought his wife, Peggy, a flock of ten mallard
ducks and set them free on the pond. Vernon would not
let Peggy sit outside during the day because the doctors
said that her skin would be extra sensitive to sunlight,
but he thought that the two of them could sit together
on the porch in the evenings, when the sun was lower
and not so dangerous, and watch the ducks swim. He
thought that Peggy might like that. He repeated it to
himself over and over as he drove home: These ducks
will be just the thing Peggy needs. These ducks are just
what the doctor ordered. The ducks squatted flat against
the bottoms of the two cages in the back of his truck.
They stretched their necks out straight and opened their
bills and hissed.

Peggy had wanted to build a house in Rutherfordton,
the next town over, after Vernon retired from Stone-
cutter Mills — they had always rented — but Vernon

insisted on buying the twenty-five acres of land he had found off Oakland Road and putting a mobile home beside the pond. He said it would be like a place in the mountains, a summer home, a cabin, that it would be good for them both to finally get out of town, out away from the noise and the traffic. But Peggy never thought it was a good idea, and did not let go easily of the idea of owning her own house. She thought that if anything she could use a little more noise and traffic. But she signed the papers anyway without telling Vernon how much she hated it.

Peggy knew that Vernon meant well. He had been saving his money for years. When his co-workers in the weave room said at his going-away lunch that he still had the first penny he ever made, he did not mind the joke. He paid cash for the land — how many of those yahoos at the mill could do that? — and he financed the mobile home for three years only. They moved into it the day after Vernon retired from the mill. The sides of the mobile home were made out of thin vinyl, and Peggy was pleased to think that at least it was not substantial, that you could put wheels on it and drag it away, that it would not last for years and years after she died, that people could not drive by and point at it after she was gone and say that it was the home of Peggy Jackson, the one thing she had wanted all of her life.

When Peggy was still a baby, her father left Spindale and took his family to California. World War II had just started and he thought that he could make his fortune working in the aircraft plants. They rented a small pink and white stucco house in a new development named Rancho Apache, on a street with stunted palm trees growing up through the strips of dry grass between the sidewalk and the pavement. The development was laid out in straight lines in a valley between two brown hills. The streets were paved with new black ribbons of thin asphalt.

The first fall Peggy and her family spent in California the Santa Ana winds pushed a brush fire down the sides of one of the hills and into the edge of Rancho Apache, where it burned five houses. Peggy's mother bought a camera to take a picture of the fire but instead took a picture of Peggy and Peggy's father beside the palm tree in front of their house. She wrote "Here We Are In Paradise" on the back of the picture and mailed it to her family back in Spindale.

One day after Peggy came home from the hospital, she looked out the kitchen window at the red dirt bank cut into the side of the hill and realized that Vernon had never known her at all. The thought came to Peggy quickly, as if a hypnotist had snapped his fingers to wake her from a deep sleep, and she knew that it was the absolute truth. Vernon had for all these years loved who he thought was Peggy, some dream of his that rode in out of the blue from California when he had just about given up. She knew that Vernon still felt about her the way he did when he first saw her, when he did not even know her name. He had always treated her like something that would shatter if he touched it very hard, something rare and beautiful that he could not believe was his and did not deserve. The front of their mobile home faced the pond, and Peggy liked the view, especially right after sunset when the water was dark and still like a mirror and the whole world seemed green and lush, but the back windows faced the red dirt bank, which was almost as tall as their trailer. She thought, *Vernon should have known better than to stick a trailer in a hole,* and she thought, *Vernon has got no right to think about me like that. It is not who I am.* When it rained, red mud from the bank washed down underneath the trailer and out the other side onto their concrete deck. Vernon had to wash the mud off with a hose. The bank was scarred with gullies. That first spring Vernon tried to plant grass on the bank, but it didn't take. There was no topsoil, only the red clay in which nothing would grow. The straw he put down washed up underneath the trailer, and birds ate the seed.

Vernon refused to look at Peggy's scars. The color drained from his face and he looked away whenever she tried to show him. She needed him to see, but he left the room when she undressed. He was not even curious about the prosthetic bras, what it felt like to wear them, how they were made, how the cups were filled with silicone that was heavy like the weight of breasts, how they were even warm when she took the bras off at night.

One night in bed she opened her pajama top and

took Vernon's hand and moved his fingers over her scars and imagined that the story of her life was written there in Braille. She thought, *This is who I am, Vernon Jackson. This is everything you need to know about me. All you have to do is read.* But the scars were still thin and Vernon's fingers seemed incapable of following them to their ends. Peggy had to guide his hand the whole time. She could tell by his touch that he did not understand what she meant at all. "I am so sorry, Peggy," he said. Whenever Vernon thought about the surgery he wanted to kill the doctor who had done it. He didn't tell anybody about it because he was afraid that they would tell him how it was wrong to feel that way, that they would try to make him feel better.

In the picture Peggy's father is wearing new aviator sunglasses and two-tone saddle shoes. He squats on his heels and holds Peggy's hands over her head — she couldn't stand by herself yet and is wearing only a diaper — and they both squint toward the camera. Peggy found the picture in a cigar box of old letters after her grandmother died. Her young father looked sad somehow, like nothing in the world but the small place in North Carolina he was trying to get away from. When she found out she was sick she dug the picture out and studied it. Her nipples were tiny and pale, like pencil marks.

Peggy's father died of lung cancer in a dark, bad-smelling hospital ward in Los Angeles with a vaporizer on the other side of the room spitting out mentholated clouds of cold steam. The walls in the hospital were green halfway up, and white up to the high ceilings, and three telephone numbers were written neatly in pencil on the wall above her father's bed. There wasn't a phone in the room, and Peggy wondered who had written the numbers there, who it was they had wanted to call and what they had wanted to say.

Peggy helped her mother bathe her father two days before he died. She was seventeen. She stood on one side of the bed and her mother stood on the other. Her father had stopped talking altogether and looked at them accusingly, moving only his eyes, wanting them to do something. The morphine had stopped doing him any good. He weighed less than a hundred pounds then, and Peggy was fascinated by how the hollows between his collarbones and his shoulders held water. She squeezed her washcloth out into the little hollow until it was filled to the top like a bowl or a lake. "Stop that," her mother said, and reached across the bed and wiped the water away with a towel.

Peggy and her mother buried her father in a cemetery in Los Angeles where precisely aligned rows of white tombstones stretched away as far as Peggy cared to look. Hardly anyone came to the funeral: a few people from the plant, a few neighbors from Rancho Apache, no one they knew very well. Peggy's mother hadn't been able to afford shipping her husband all the way back to North Carolina, which she had promised him she would do. When she died of lymphomatosis twenty years later she still felt guilty. Peggy's mother couldn't pay the hospital bills, and she and Peggy moved back to Spindale suddenly. They took a train east one morning before the sun came up, and did not leave a forwarding address. "We never belonged here, Peggy," her mother said. "We never should've come."

The ducks huddled together on the bank. Their low clucks and grunts sounded, to Vernon, like questions. He put the empty cages back into the bed of his truck and tried to shoo the ducks into the pond. He promised them that they would be happy there, that he would feed them yellow corn every day, that all they had to do in this world was swim for Peggy, but they would not go into the water. They waddled away from him and squawked and flapped their wings every time he got too close. They moved in circles around and around him, and in the late-afternoon light the luminous, dark heads of the drakes changed from green to blue to purple to black.

The pink and white house Peggy grew up in in California was identical to the one across the street from it. When Peggy was a little girl she used to go out into the middle of the street and close her eyes and spin around until she got so dizzy that she felt like she was standing on the side of a wall. Then she would spin a few turns in the other direction and open her eyes and, as the world revolved around her, try to guess which house was hers. Sometimes Peggy guessed wrong, and picked the wrong house, and then her house didn't feel like her house for the rest of the day. She felt as if everything she knew had been packed up while she was asleep and carried to the wrong side of the street, as if she were a different person than who her parents thought she was, as if nothing she knew were real.

The morning before Peggy was supposed to go home from the hospital, Vernon spread orange marmalade on her toast because she was still too sore from the surgery to raise her arms for very long at a time. Vernon told her that he was thinking about buying her a flock of ducks for the pond, and about how pretty they would be swimming on the green water. He told her that their wings would be clipped so they could not fly. He asked her if she would like that, if she would like watching her own flock of ducks swim on the pond.

Vernon seemed so excited about the idea that Peggy didn't tell him that she had never thought much about ducks one way or the other, that she did not think they would help, that at the moment she did not think that anything would help, that she could feel cancer cells hanging around outside her organs like looters waiting for dark. Peggy was so shy when they first met that she did not think she had anything to say. And later, when she realized that she did have things to say, it seemed much too late to suddenly start talking. The nurse came in and took the green plastic basin out from under the sink and winked at Peggy and asked Vernon if he would like to give Mrs. Jackson a bath. Vernon's face went white and angry and he mumbled something that neither the nurse nor Peggy could understand, some kind of apology, and left the room. After the nurse removed Peggy's gown, Peggy slowly raised and crossed her arms and ran a finger down the length of each collarbone.

Vernon met Peggy at a mill-sponsored square dance at the Spindale House. She had just enrolled at R-S Central for her senior year. Her mother was still wearing black. Vernon was tall and broad-shouldered, strong-looking, but with a narrow waist and a high round butt, and when he came into the gym Peggy noticed how everybody he passed spoke to him, how the men all wanted to shake his hand. Five or six small boys followed him around and tried to walk the way he walked. She also thought he was ugly — his nose was long and sharp and his black eyes were too small and too close together — and during all the years they were married she never changed her opinion much.

Vernon was the ace pitcher for the Rutherford County Owls semiprofessional baseball team, and had been for as long as Peggy had been alive. Peggy's father had even played a little mill-league baseball with him. The Cincinnati Reds once paid Vernon an eight-thousand-dollar bonus simply to sign a professional contract, but he got homesick during the first week of spring training in Florida and came back to Spindale. He gave the money back to the Reds and spent the rest of his baseball career pitching against the semipro teams from Shelby and Cherryville and Lincolnton and Kings Mountain.

Vernon was thirty-two when he saw Peggy at the square dance, and he thought that she was the most beautiful girl he had ever seen. Nobody in California had ever thought that about Peggy — she knew she wasn't particularly pretty — so after she got to know Vernon she decided to let him think that way if he wanted to. Peggy was so petite that Vernon knew he could pick her up with one arm and raise her over his head. He stood close behind her and pretended to watch the band, but strained to listen as she talked to her mother. She had a California accent, which Vernon thought was sophisticated and exotic. In his mind he measured the new girl against his body and decided that she couldn't be more than five feet two or three. As Vernon stood there, almost close enough to smell her, he was filled with a desperation bordering on despair, a longing to keep anyone else from ever talking to her and marrying her before he could.

Peggy and Vernon created quite a stir at the square dance. Nobody in Spindale had ever seen Vernon Jackson talk to a girl, much less dance with one. When he walked out onto the gym floor with Peggy, people pointed and whispered about how Old Vernon must be in love with the new girl. The caller saw what was going on and directed all of the dance instructions specifically at Vernon: Bow to your partner, Vernon. Now bow to your corner gal. When they skipped around the floor, part of a circle so large that the wind from it blew the paper streamers hanging from the ceiling, Peggy noticed how everybody smiled as they passed. She decided that she liked being seen with Vernon, even if he was ugly.

Vernon decided that he was absolutely in love with Peggy a week later when he saw her climb into the old covered bleachers behind home plate at Legion Field in Forest City. The Owls were playing Bessemer City that night, and Vernon was so nervous that he walked the first three batters he faced, which was unheard of because he was known for his control. Once on a bet he stood on one side of Main Street and threw a baseball through the two open windows of a moving car.

With the bases loaded, and Bessemer City's cleanup man at the plate, Vernon stood behind the mound and rubbed the baseball. He was shaking inside, the way he had in Florida. The baseball felt strange in his hands. He was afraid of where it might go if he threw it again. He looked out from underneath the bill of his cap and up into the stands and found Peggy — she was wearing a blue jumper and saddle shoes, and she had a sweater around her shoulders even though it was a muggy night — and he thought that he could feel her pulling for him, wanting him to do well. He looked at her and rubbed the ball until he was sure of it. He imagined that maybe, just maybe, she loved him too, and that was why she had come to the game.

Vernon had never been in love before and he pounded the baseball into the pocket of his glove and considered what it meant. He thought about how the chicken-wire backstop was rusty and rotten and how sometimes foul balls sailed right through it and into the bleachers. He stepped back up on the mound and threw a pitch at the head of the Bessemer City cleanup man for even thinking about touching the baseball with a bat, and then he struck him out on three pitches. Vernon looked into the bleachers and tipped his cap to Peggy. Then he struck out the next two batters as well. Later the Bessemer City pitcher, who did not know that Vernon was in love, threw a pitch at Vernon's head for being arrogant.

By the time school started two weeks later, the new girl from California was also known as Vernon Jackson's girl, which Peggy did not mind because it spared her having to make friends. It seemed like everybody was already her friend. Vernon helped coach the Central baseball team, and although she did not know any of the players — she had been in school less than a month — they voted her their homecoming sponsor. Her mother and grandmother stayed up late and made her a lavender taffeta dress, which she wore in the parade down the Main Streets of Spindale and Rutherfordton. Peggy didn't mind riding through Spindale because the street was wide and the crowd wasn't that big, but in Rutherfordton the sidewalks were packed to the point that people spilled out into the street, almost close enough for Peggy to touch. Everyone seemed happy to see her, and hundreds of people waved at her, although she didn't see a single face she had ever seen before. They all seemed to want something from her, but she could not for the life of her figure out what.

Peggy always enjoyed watching Vernon pitch, although it embarrassed her — and later made her mad — whenever he tipped his cap to her after a strikeout. After it got to be a tradition, people in the bleachers turned around and looked at her, waiting to see her reaction. She always smiled and clapped, and meant it, but she resented people expecting it. She thought it should be her business whether she smiled at Vernon or not. On game days people she didn't even know used to yell out all the way across Main Street, Hey, Peggy, How Many Is Old Vernon Going To Strike Out Tonight?

Whenever Vernon went into his windup he drew his right leg up in front of him, like a flamingo — he was a southpaw — with his knee up tight against his chest. He leaned slowly back, extending his leg and raising his foot high over his head. Just when it looked like he was going to fall over backward, he strode toward home plate so far that he looked like he was going to step over it. His left knee dragged the ground. His arm whipped in a blur up over his head and down across his body, and his left leg flew up in the air behind him. He threw the ball so hard that it never looked to Peggy like anything more than a white streak. She didn't see how anybody ever managed to hit it. She loved the violent sound of Vernon's fastball hitting the catcher's mitt. She didn't like it when he threw curves or change-ups because they sounded like mistakes. Later, when they were trying to have children — and they tried for years — Peggy imagined Vernon's sperm to be baseballs traveling inside her at great velocity, and in her imagination tried to catch one, just one, and hold on to it.

Peggy had heard people tell stories about phantom limbs, about amputees trying to scratch arms and legs that had been cut off years before. She never missed her breasts like that — it did not ever *feel* to her like they were still there; even the first day after the surgery it felt like they were simply *gone* — but sometimes what she could imagine was the touch of Vernon's big hands. Vernon was a gentle man, but he did like to squeeze her breasts — he squeezed them when they made love until her nipples were so stiff and erect that she was surprised they didn't hum, and sometimes she found bruises on her breasts in the shape of his fingertips — and she wondered if over the years he had hurt her somehow.

Vernon and Peggy went up and over the mountains on Highway 74 to Asheville on their honeymoon. They stayed at the old Biltmore Hotel, which by that time was shabby, although Vernon didn't seem to notice. Their mattress smelled moldy, and faint pathways were worn into the red carpet in the hallways. The oscillating fan in the window of their room was broken and it lay on its side and rattled and blew air in only one direction.

The first night they ate dinner at the S&W Cafeteria and saw *Giant* with James Dean at the Plaza Theatre. They went to their room and undressed with the lights out. Peggy had never thought much about what a big man Vernon was until he climbed into the bed and covered her small body with his own large one. She thought that if God were looking down on them, he wouldn't be able to see her at all.

Peggy was relieved and glad that she was excited about making love, that she liked how it felt being naked with Vernon, the way her skin felt against his, that she was wet — she had been afraid she wouldn't be because her mother had given her a jar of Vaseline to put in her overnight bag, just in case — but it still hurt when he tried to put himself inside her. When she gasped Vernon jumped up and sat up on the edge of the bed with his head in his hands and refused to try again the rest of the night. She desperately wanted him to finish it, but she did not say anything. She knew already that it was easier not to tell Vernon things he wouldn't understand. On one of their first dates he asked her if all the girls in California were as pretty as she was and when she laughed he didn't understand why. He blushed and looked away and didn't say anything for a long time.

Peggy did not lose her virginity until two nights after her wedding night — after they had toured the Biltmore House twice, and driven all the way to Mount Mitchell on the Parkway, had a fried-chicken picnic on the lawn of the Grove Park Inn, and sat in the car on Beaucatcher

Mountain and looked out over Asheville and drank Coca-Colas and listened to the Game of the Week on the radio — because he was so afraid of hurting her. Peggy had wanted to scream, "Just do it, Vernon. Just shut up, just stop apologizing and do it and get it over with. I want to do it as much as you do. Just who in the hell do you think you are?" When the membrane finally started to tear Peggy had to put her hands on Vernon's buttocks and push him down hard to make him break through. The next morning he was terrified by the blood on the sheets and wanted to hide them from the maid. He didn't talk much during breakfast, and all the way down the mountain toward home he patted her knee like she was broken. Peggy put her hand on the inside of Vernon's leg, up close to his crotch, and left it there all the way to Spindale even though she saw that it made him uncomfortable.

Even after Vernon and Peggy had been married twenty-five years, and he hadn't touched a baseball in twenty, people used to come up to them in Scoggin's or Inland Harbor and tell Vernon how he would have been a star in the pros, how he would've been in the Hall of Fame by now. Vernon always told them how marrying Peggy had been more important to him than pitching baseballs. Peggy knew that Vernon meant it — and meant it as a compliment to her — but every time he said it she wanted to stand up on a chair and announce that the one time Vernon Jackson had gone to spring training in Florida she had been three years old, and lived in California with her parents, and that none of it, absolutely none of it, had been her fault. Throwing a baseball had been the one thing Vernon did magnificently, the one thing he had been born to do. It was what made him different, and Peggy didn't think that he had ever understood the importance of his gift. All he had been after he quit pitching baseball was just a good man. That was all. Just another good man. The mills in Spindale were crawling with men like that.

Almost all of Peggy's hair came out at once. She stood in front of the mirror in the bathroom of the trailer and pulled it out by the handful. It didn't hurt at all. That was the amazing thing. Vernon went into the bathroom and got all of the hair out of the trash can, and all the hair out of her brush, and put it in an envelope. When she yelled at him and called him stupid he staggered backward and left in the truck and drove up Highway 74 into the mountains. He stopped in Gerton and called her collect from a phone booth and cried and told her how much he loved her and how he didn't want her to ever die. She told Vernon that she loved him too and to please come back, that she had yelled at him because she was sick. On the way home he turned off of the highway onto the bridge on Rock Springs Road and emptied the envelope of Peggy's hair into the dark river running below. Vernon cried instantly, and for a long time, wishing that he had saved Peggy's hair.

*   *   *

Soon after that Peggy started to think that everything
was funny. Sometimes, when she wasn't even thinking
about anything in particular, a single, loud giggle would
bubble up and force itself out of her mouth. It happened
one Sunday in church, during a sermon about Shadrack,
Meshack, and Abednego — it was those silly names that
did it — and everyone turned around and looked at
her with such sympathy — they thought something was
wrong with *her*, not with those names — that she broke
out laughing uncontrollably and had to leave the
church. One day Peggy lathered up her head with Vernon's shaving cream and shaved off the few strands of
hair she had left. Vernon said that she should wear a hat
to keep from catching a cold, so she knitted herself a
bright red ski cap with a big ball on top. She sent Vernon
out for more yarn so that she could make it longer. She
tacked a paper cone inside the hat so that it would stand
up straight. It was a ridiculous hat and it made her laugh
to wear it. It was over a foot tall. It made her almost as
tall as Vernon. It looked like a siren. Sometimes she sat
outside in her pointy red hat with her new silicone
breasts strapped on — they even had *nipples* — and
watched Vernon's ducks swimming and humping each
other and laughed until her sides hurt. Vernon called
Peggy's doctor and told him that Peggy was becoming
hysterical. The doctor prescribed some pills, but Peggy
wouldn't take them. The last thing she wanted to do,
besides vomit ever again, was take more pills. Vernon
brought her a wig to wear when they went out to eat,

and she wore it, but she did not like to. It was made out of nylon, and it itched and did not feel or look like hair.

Peggy came to like the way her head felt bald, especially when she stood under the stream of hot water in the shower. She told Vernon that rubbing it would bring him good luck, but he refused. He said that it would work only if she was a catcher. Whenever she touched her smooth head, it somehow said more to her about who she was than any of her hairdos ever had. She liked the way it looked, too. The web of veins beneath the skin of her scalp was a delicate blue, like the lines on a map, the color of expensive eye shadow.

One day Peggy found a scar that she had forgotten she had. As soon as she touched the scar, she smelled the house in California she had grown up in as plainly as if she had been standing in it. She remembered being very young and running across the kitchen floor, which her mother kept waxed slick, and slipping and falling and hitting her head against the edge of the table. She couldn't remember where her mother was, but her father took her to the hospital, where she got three stitches and a green sucker. After that he drove her over the brown hills and down to the ocean. He took off his saddle shoes and tied the laces together and rolled up the cuffs of his pants and carried her on his shoulders across the sand.

From the top of one of the hills on the way home she saw the tall buildings of downtown Los Angeles sprouting up in the distance. Peggy knew when she found the memory that it had to be the first time she had noticed the city. The sun glinted orange off of the windows, and at first she thought the buildings were on fire. Her father sat with one of his hands lightly draped on the back of her neck, and softly sang, Ruby, honey are you mad at your man, the song that always made her mother cry because it reminded her of home, and Peggy thought that somehow her daddy had made the buildings glow just for her. She slid up close to him and smelled Old Spice and tobacco. He always kept a pack of Lucky Strikes in the pocket of his shirt. The wind was cool and it blew her long hair, and she felt it tickling her father's face. She had forgotten all of it.

Peggy and Vernon's only child was stillborn. She had known from the beginning of her pregnancy that something was terribly wrong. She woke with a gasp the night she conceived and listened because she thought somebody had broken into the house. Her mother told her it was nerves. Vernon talked constantly about teaching their son how to make a fastball break in on a right-handed batter and about not letting him throw curves until he was good and strong, until his legs were as big around as fence posts. Their son, he said, would stick it out in the pros. Peggy tried, but could not imagine their son at all. The baby — they were going to name it Charlie, after her father, although only Vernon ever called it that; she didn't like to call it anything — grew too fast, demanded too much of her, and grew so big by the eighth month that Peggy could hardly walk. When the baby moved inside her it felt desperate somehow, almost as if it knew she was incapable of giving it birth.

When Peggy went into labor she told Dr. Keeter that she wanted him to deliver the baby by cesarean section. He laughed and said that it wouldn't be necessary, that she and the child would both be fine, that they were both healthy and strong. He had a mask tied around his neck, and Peggy wanted to poke his eyes out with her fingers. She was in labor for thirty-six hours, gagging, the room spinning, from the shots they gave her. She almost bled to death. They poured bottles of blood into her the whole time. They couldn't operate because she was bleeding. She thought the baby was going to rip her apart. It was huge, a boy, and bright blue. Dr. Keeter carried it to a small table on one side of the delivery room and blew into its mouth, but he couldn't save it.

Vernon cried when he saw Peggy and leaned over her bed and brushed her hair with his hand and told her that it was all his fault, that "you can't breed an ugly old Brahma bull with a pretty little Jersey cow because the calf would be too big," and that he should've known better and shouldn't have done such a terrible, terrible thing to her. It was several months after that before Peggy could even stand the sight of Vernon, before she got over the urge to beat him with her fists every time he walked into the room, and a while after that before she let him touch her.

The ducks weren't mated pairs and they bred randomly. The drakes fought among themselves and chased the

hens back and forth across the pond. One afternoon
Peggy and Vernon watched three of the drakes take
turns on top of the smallest hen. Peggy wore her pointed
red hat. It was all she could do to keep from laughing
out loud. One at a time each of the drakes hovered
above the hen with its wings flapping, pushing the hen
underneath the water. They beat the water into a froth
with their wings and reached forward with their long
necks and bit at the back of the hen, quacking like mad
the whole time. Sometimes Peggy and Vernon couldn't
see the hen at all. The whole flock pointed their bills at
the air and flapped their wings and raised hell like they
did at feeding time. Each time the hen got free it tried to
get away, only to be chased down and mounted by
another drake. Peggy thought, *I wish Vernon would
fuck me like that.* She had never used that word before.
She handled it like a lump. *Fuck, fuck, fuck me, Vernon.*
The third drake mounted the hen. Peggy glanced over at
Vernon and put her hand over her mouth to keep from
saying "Fuck me." Vernon swallowed and would not
look at her. A mud turtle materialized in the water
behind the two ducks and with its terrible jaws attached
itself to the struggling hen. The hen screamed like an
infant crying and whipped its neck from side to side
against the water. Peggy reached up and jerked off her
red cap and twisted it in her hands. She felt the paper
cone crumple inside it. The drakes beat their clipped
wings against the surface of the pond and tried to fly
away. The hen swam in smaller and smaller circles,
crying out — the turtle pulling it down — its head

barely above the water, and then finally disappeared. It floated back to the surface ten minutes later, the water slick around it. Five turtles rose to the surface of the pond then, appeared like round shadows in the water, their heads black and erect, and latched on to the hen's still body.

Vernon ran into the trailer and came back out with his deer rifle. He braced himself against the side of the trailer, sighted down the barrel at the back of the largest turtle, and pulled the trigger. A geyser of water and pieces of shell flew into the air. "You son-of-a-bitch," screamed Vernon. "You stinking bastard son-of-a-bitch." The other four turtles sank out of sight before he could shoot again. Peggy jumped in her chair and clapped her hands, thrilled by the ringing boom of the rifle and the echo of the shot off of the distant mountains, the language Vernon had used and the way he had shouted it. It was the most noise she had heard in months. Vernon was as quiet as a mouse around her. And polite. He actually *tiptoed*. Sometimes she wanted to smack him, just to make him mad. She wanted Vernon to shoot the rifle again, even though the turtles were gone.

Vernon bought a picnic table and placed it so that it faced the pond. He filled a sandbag and put it on top of the table. He used the sandbag as a support for the rifle when he shot turtles. Vernon kept a steady watch most of the time and killed three more turtles during the course of the summer. The turtles became wary. If Vernon did not lever a shell into the rifle before he came outside, they would disappear from sight the instant they heard the noise. The turtles meanwhile killed five more ducks. The rest of the ducks stayed in the pond less and less. Foxes killed three while they walked on the bank. Peggy and Vernon's last duck was a drake. It stood in the edge of the water and flapped its wings and quacked questions Vernon couldn't answer, until he thought that his heart was going to break. "I think we should name that duck," Peggy said.

"No we shouldn't," Vernon said. "I don't want to."

"We shouldn't have bought ducks with clipped wings," she said.

Vernon shook his head. He avoided looking at Peggy's eyes. "Then they would have flown away."

"That would've been a good thing," she said.

The first frosty morning of fall Peggy found swollen lymph nodes in her neck and underneath each armpit. That was it. The looters were carrying her life out under their arms like television sets. Peggy's hair had come back delicate and fine like a baby's, and it was white as snow. She put a red barrette in it. She had stopped wearing her pointy hat and — except for when they went out to eat — her prosthesis. Vernon still sat at the picnic table, but he hadn't seen a turtle in days, and she had noticed that lately he stared into space as much as he stared at the pond. Peggy wasn't scared, not in a way she could explain — some days it wasn't scary at all, which surprised her; she felt excited more than anything else, almost as if she were going on a trip; they had sold her father's car and ridden trains all the way back to North Carolina and she had always wanted to do it again — she just dreaded being sick. Being sick was something that had to be gotten through, like Arizona and New Mexico and Texas, to get to the thing on the other side. Sometimes she hyperventilated a little thinking about it, but she couldn't exactly call it being scared. It was more like standing, with nothing to hold on to, on top of something very tall.

Peggy wanted to tell Vernon something. She wanted to sum up her life from the first things she knew — the pink and white house, the buildings in the sun, the way Lucky Strikes and Old Spice smelled on her father — and tell him everything that had happened up until now, every single thing she could remember and what it had all meant. She stared at his back a long time and said, "I just want you to know that I'm different than you are, Vernon."

Vernon turned around and looked at her and smiled. He had been watching the pond. "I know you are," he said. "You're from California."

"That's right," she said. "I am." That wasn't exactly true, Peggy knew — she had been born on Spindale Street, four doors down from Keller's Cafe — but she decided that it was close enough. Their last duck swam close to the bank. Its reflection swam through trees underneath it in the green water. Peggy pointed at the pond. "That's as pretty as a new baseball, isn't it?" she said.

"It sure is," Vernon said. "Official Major League. Straight out of the box." He scanned the lake. Their duck was the only thing moving on the water. "I think the old boy is going to make it," he said. "I haven't seen any turtles in a long time."

"I'm sure he's going to make it," Peggy said. "He's a smart one. He's going to be fine."

"I'm thinking about getting some more ducks in the spring," Vernon said. "I'm thinking about getting you a whole new flock of ducks. Maybe some Canadian geese."

"I'd like that, Vernon," she said.

Peggy remembered watching the three drakes mount the hen, and as she remembered the word *fuck* rose inside her like a bubble — so close to the surface that she could taste the hard, salty word, rich inside her mouth. But she knew that Vernon would not understand what she needed, even if she said it out loud. Vernon loved her too much. That was all there was to it, and she would not hurt him by saying it. The pond was still full of snapping turtles — they had buried themselves in the mud in the deepest part of the pond and waited only for spring — but she did not want him to know. Peggy looked all around her and supposed that it had been a good enough way to live.

GETTYSBURG

WHEN TULLY ARRIVED in Gettysburg, at his friend Frank's house, he found Frank perched on a stepladder, in yellow elbow-length rubber gloves, removing baby birds from the rain guttering. Frank's girlfriend, Eileen, stood beneath him, holding a shoebox, on one of the ladder's lower rungs. Eileen, too, wore yellow rubber gloves. She was tiny, less than five feet tall, and her gloves reached significantly past her elbows, which made them look oddly formal. Eileen was pretty, and noticeably younger than Frank, as Tully had known she would be. He guessed that she was twenty-five or twenty-six. Frank had been dating women that age, all of them pretty, for the last fifteen years. Eileen's nose and cheeks were sprinkled with adult freckles, and a wild tangle of thick, brown hair fell down around her shoulders. Tully had noted that in commercials for shampoo and makeup famous models now wore their hair like that. Eileen was the first woman Tully had seen who wore her hair like that in real life.

Eileen spotted Tully on the sidewalk before he had a chance to speak, and Tully hoped she didn't think he had tried to look up her shorts. Because he hadn't. Although he could have. The ladder was balanced somewhat dangerously on the top step of the front porch, which made not looking up Eileen's shorts difficult. Once upon a time he would have looked, certainly, but not anymore. Tully was a changed man, and already felt compelled to explain himself. Eileen's eyes were so blue that Tully wondered if she wore contacts. She smiled and greeted him with an exaggerated yellow wave. "You must be Tully," she said. "I'm Eileen. Frank made me wear these stupid gloves." Tully nodded and self-consciously returned her smile. Eileen's brown legs disappeared into her baggy soccer shorts everywhere he seemed to look. Frank turned on the ladder until he faced Tully. He held his hands out in front of him, fingers pointed up, doctor-style, as if removing baby birds from a rain gutter were a sterile procedure. Tully didn't know if Frank was joking or not. It was always hard to tell with Frank. "Tully," Frank said, "settle this. Yes or no. Do you think that baby birds might have germs on them?"

Tully was still stupid with driving, and would have been content to stand in the sunshine on the sidewalk and nod pleasantly. He was not yet used to the idea of being in Gettysburg, Pennsylvania, a place he had heard about all his life but had never visited before, and didn't want to answer any difficult questions. He was still disconcerted from having traveled almost all the way through the rolling fields on the west side of town before realizing they were part of the battlefield. Tully was disappointed with himself, not only because he didn't get a good look, but because he had bought and read a book on the battle in preparation for his trip, and still didn't recognize any of the landmarks he had studied on the maps and in the old photographs of the dead. Instead he had been startled by an obelisk on top of a hill to his left, a monument of some kind, incongruous as a spaceship in the middle of what he had assumed was a farm. Then he realized that the fields on both sides of the highway were dotted with such monuments, with cannons and bronze generals on horseback and the split-rail fences of postcards, and before he could savor the revelation that he was crossing historic ground, and formally think some appropriate thought, one he would always recall, he was through the park and into the town itself.

Gettysburg was clean and well-kept, and decorated for tourists in much the same way hunters might decorate a field in the hopes of attracting passing geese. Tully lived in such a town in North Carolina and recognized instantly the souvenir shops and wax museums and miniature golf courses and brightly painted theme restaurants that only people suffering the insanity of vacation would consider entering, and as he negotiated the thick, slightly addled sight-seeing traffic downtown, he felt a little of the irritation he experienced at home whenever he found himself held up on a mountain road behind a slow-moving Lincoln with Florida plates. Tully draped his arm out the window as he circled the square and arranged on his face a stern look of boredom and purpose, which he hoped would allow the locals to identify him as one of them, a townie from another town, a man with things to do, whose patience was tried daily by tourists. He also thought that he should be exempt from whatever derision his out-of-state license plate might draw from the locals because three of his ancestors, three brothers on his mother's side, had fought at Gettysburg for the Confederacy. His great-great-grandfather William Womack had been shot through the arm, and William's brother John had disappeared in the chaos of the battle and was never heard from again. Only the third brother, Anderson, made it home unscathed. Tully fancied himself on some sort of historical rescue mission — he harbored a vague notion of somehow *finding* Uncle John — and therefore believed that at least *his* presence in Gettysburg was justified.

"Germs or not?" Frank said.

"What kind of birds are they?"

"Chimney sweeps."

"Swifts," said Eileen. "They're swifts."

"Whatever," said Frank.

"I don't know," Tully said. "It's hard to tell with chimney swifts. It depends on the chimney."

"You always were a smart ass, Tully," Frank said. "Did you know that I can see your bald spot from here?"

"Hah!" Eileen almost shouted. "It depends on the chimney. Hah!"

Eileen appeared genuinely delighted with Tully's

answer, which made him blush. He liked it when people thought he was witty, although caring whether or not people thought he was witty, as well as people occasionally thinking that he was, were both fairly recent developments. Tully was one of those men who had early on defined himself in strictly physical terms — he was a wide-shouldered and strong six feet eight, and had been an outstanding high school basketball player — and most of his life had been content to live in relative isolation inside the rather large space occupied by his body. Until recently he had talked little more than was necessary, and never liked being pressed into conversation. But now he regularly surprised himself by talking to strangers in Shoney's. His head had become filled, to the point of insomnia, with ideas and questions and a need to explain something, although he didn't know what, a condition that perplexed him. Tully had no idea who he was anymore. He felt brand-new and untested, as if he were fluently speaking a foreign language in a dream, but wasn't quite sure what he was saying.

He had been to his cousin Tina's wedding in a New Jersey suburb, and was on his way back to North Carolina, where — he wanted to tell someone, because it showed he had priorities — he loved his wife and sold real estate. Tully thought of this new definition of himself on the drive up, on the interstate in Virginia, beside the long, low mountain named for Stonewall Jackson. Tully had been lovesick for his wife at the time — another new development, he and Crystal had been married eighteen years, and although their marriage was a good one, with no diagnosed terminal illnesses, Tully inexplicably felt most of the time as if his heart were breaking — and somehow Jackson's famous last words, "Let us cross over the river, and rest in the shade of the trees," had transformed themselves into the more personal declaration that had for the rest of his trip thumped inside his head like a bad tire. Tully knew his declaration lacked the mystical grandeur of Jackson's, and over the previous few days had grown a little tired of it, but he nonetheless considered it worthy of remembering and possible use. In New Jersey he imagined breathing the words "I love my wife, and I sell real estate" to a teary-eyed state trooper, beside some anonymous northern highway, while firemen frantically worked to free him from the wreckage of his car. He believed there was a better than average chance he would use the words to describe himself, should anyone ask. But so far, no one on the trip had. In New Jersey, he had been Tina's cousin Tully from North Carolina. That was all anyone had wanted to know. He carried his unused declaration inside him like a mine, or a song.

"What are those birds doing in the gutter?" Tully said.

"Frank put them there."

"I made a mistake. So I'm not a freaking biologist." Frank turned away and stared again at whatever dilemma faced him in the guttering.

"He tried to cook them," Eileen said. "In the *sun*."

"Get off it, already," Frank said. "I'm tired of hearing about it."

Eileen directed a smirk upward at Frank and then told the story. Frank had been watching television that morning when the nest containing the three birds fell down the chimney and into the fireplace. Eileen, whose degrees were in marine biology, but at least knew ornithologists, had been out. Left to his own devices, Frank borrowed a stepladder from a neighbor, secured gloves from beneath the kitchen sink, and placed the squawking birds in the guttering. He mistakenly thought the birds' parents would rescue them. The hatchlings had been in the sun for a couple of hours before Eileen came home. This is where Tully showed up. He felt late, a policeman arrived on the scene long after other policemen had sealed off the area with yellow tape and interviewed all the important witnesses. He wanted to do something helpful, and was grateful when Frank asked him to see if birds were still flying in and out of the chimney. Tully backed toward the street, shielded his eyes with his hand, and looked up. He was surprised when a bird did, in fact, fly into the chimney. Before he could say anything another bird flew out. Or maybe it was the same bird. Tully really couldn't say. Everything seemed mysterious and urgent. He watched the second bird disappear behind the house next door. "They're still up there," he said, startled by the loudness of his voice, and once again disappointed with himself. That hadn't been helpful at all.

Eileen, however, thought Tully was making fun of Frank, and when she smiled in approval Tully didn't correct her. She held out one of her arms for Tully's benefit and stared with exaggerated disdain at the yellow glove. Tully was happy that Eileen was a marine biologist, and hoped he would get a chance to ask her about the things she knew. He had recently become impressed with acquired knowledge, and had started watching documentaries on cable. He browsed in the history and science sections of the bookstore at the mall, and accidentally memorized odd facts. The Chinese in Tibet worried him. Many types of lemurs were disappearing from the earth. He pictured Eileen scuba diving, studying something. Coral maybe. Tully didn't know anything about coral, so he couldn't picture it for very long. He thought that there was something dangerous about it, but he couldn't remember what it was. Maybe it was sharp. He didn't think coral was poisonous. He wondered if Eileen was big enough to swim with an air tank on her back, and if air tanks came in different sizes. Tully made a face like he smelled something dead and shook his head in commiseration: Frank *was* stupid. His surplus knowledge had formed ranks of sentences inside his head. One hundred and seventy-two thousand men had fought at Gettysburg, with fifty-one thousand casualties. On the third day Lee should have attacked the Union left flank. Frank wouldn't care. Eileen, however, was a *scientist*, unafraid to touch the live things of the earth, and Tully wanted to be on her side.

"It was a calamity of birds," Eileen said from the ladder.

"What does that mean, 'a calamity of birds'?" Frank asked. "Why do you always say things like that?" Frank leaned toward Eileen and placed something small in the shoebox.

"Because that's what it was, Frank. It was a calamity of birds."

Frank and Eileen lived in an old, but not historic, redbrick house on Lincoln Avenue, an address that pleased Tully more than he could say without embarrassing himself. The neighborhood was as pleasant as the set of an old television show — the yards had big, leafy trees, oaks and maples, the houses, deep porches — and it was a couple of blocks from Gettysburg College, where Frank was Assistant Vice-President of Development. Frank had been a development officer at several different schools in Florida, but never a vice-president before. He bought a Saab in celebration, although he and Eileen still lived in a rented house. Frank told Tully on the phone he was looking for a place to buy, but Tully knew better. Frank was one of those men who traveled light. Tully hated to see the type walk into his office. The women they were with were invariably nicer, and inevitably disappointed. No place was ever good enough for men like Frank. In Gettysburg Frank was in charge of the college's board of church visitors. It was his job, he said, to suck money out of Lutherans and make them like it. Tully hadn't seen Frank in four or five years. The last time had been in Tampa. Frank worked at the University of South Florida then, where he had said it was his job to suck money out of Jews and make them like it. There had been another girlfriend, a big one who lifted weights and drank straight tequila and cursed a lot. Tully hadn't liked her. They went deep-sea fishing and the girl ate half a bucket of Kentucky Fried Chicken and threw up into the gulf.

When Eileen climbed down off the ladder, Tully felt momentarily dizzy, as if the world had suddenly shrunk in scale around him. She was *tiny,* but perfectly proportioned, like a tall person who had been xerographically reduced. She was long-legged, but at the same time the shortest grown person Tully had ever known; she was full-figured, even chesty, but her breasts were girlishly small. She was confusing to look at. Something about her tininess was extremely attractive, and Tully thought it must have something to do with how easy it would be to pick her up and carry her around. She couldn't weigh more than eighty-five or ninety pounds. Tully had to shop in big and tall men's stores, where it was hard to find pants with belt loops, or anything made out of wool. Frank was almost as big as Tully — only two inches shorter and almost as heavy — and the difference in size between him and Eileen raised obvious, but indelicate, questions that Tully tried not to think about. Tully and Frank had been best friends and mediocre athletes together at the University of North Carolina. They became best friends their sophomore year, after they realized they would not be the stars in college they had been in high school, and diverted their attention instead to chasing girls and drinking beer. Almost twenty years later Frank still had his linebacker's cruel neck. Tully had played basketball for coach Dean Smith, a fact of which he was still proud, although during his three years on the Carolina varsity he had scored a total of eighteen points, seven of them during a particularly messy rout of Furman his senior year. Tully figured that he and Frank together were a little over thirteen feet tall, or eight feet taller than Eileen.

Two of the three chimney swifts Frank placed in the gutter had survived, at least for the moment, and Eileen stepped toward Tully with the shoebox extended so he could have a look. Frank tossed the third swift over Tully's head down into the thick grass of the front yard, where it promptly disappeared from sight. Eileen's rubber gloves looked like immense yellow arms that had been stitched to her body — the arms of a cartoon character whose job was slapping other cartoon characters — and Tully thought they looked a little dangerous. The fingers of the gloves were bent at odd angles, and he thought briefly, and with a slight, illicit twinge, about Eileen's small hands. "Do you want to see the babies?" she said. Tully felt monstrous, a sensation he had often experienced, but never quite so profoundly, around people significantly smaller than he was. The house Eileen lived in seemed impossibly large. The sidewalk she stood on was far too wide. Tully felt like he could step on an automobile and crush it. He gazed down from a great height at the two minute creatures in the box, and wouldn't have immediately considered calling them birds. They didn't look like birds at all. They were fetal and grotesque, featherless, with long, serpentine necks and scaly claws that seemed much too big for their bodies. Their eyes were closed, or filmed over, and their heads rested on the bottom of the box, as if they didn't have the strength to raise them. They seemed to be panting, and Tully thought they looked sunburned. They were a little pink, which probably wasn't a good sign. "I don't think they're going to make it," he said, feeling suddenly expert. He had watched a lot of nature shows.

"Bird toast," Eileen said. "Order up."

"Bird toast," said Frank.

Frank returned the ladder next door, and then sat on the steps between Eileen and Tully and fed the birds sugared water with a converted eyedropper. He held the birds upside down, and they craned their necks upward and squawked when he didn't squeeze the drops out fast enough. Frank learned the trick when he called the hotline number of Pennsylvanians Assisting Wildlife for instructions. The PAW volunteer told Frank that chimney swifts spent most of their lives hanging upside down, and might not eat any other way. Frank used the acronym unashamedly, and with a certain professional pride that made Eileen snicker. Tully thought that if he were a bird he would want to be something more conventional, a cardinal maybe, or a robin, although he thought that robins were vaguely disreputable, like timeshare salesmen. Tully didn't want to hang upside down, especially in the dark.

"Fwank cawed PAW," Eileen said, and after a beat snorted loudly.

"C'mon, Eileen," Frank said. "Please."

"PAW said, 'Bwing dem wight away.'"

"You're a ditz," Frank said.

Eileen elbowed Frank in the ribs, a little sharply, Tully thought. "Fwankie's a wascally wabbit," she said.

"Tully," Frank said, "you won't believe this, but down in Florida I used to do the backstroke out in the gulf with her sitting on my chest."

"But we don't swim anymore, do we, honey?" Eileen said.

"That's right," Frank said. "We don't."

Frank insisted on taking the baby birds to PAW headquarters in Harrisburg by himself, and left Eileen to show Tully around town. Before Frank left, he and Eileen argued briefly behind a closed door inside the house. Tully stayed where he was on the porch and tried not to eavesdrop. He figured it was probably his fault. He was helped in his not listening by a blue and white double-deck bus that groaned loudly up Lincoln Avenue toward the college. The bus's second level was uncovered, as if the roof had been sheared off in an accident. The exposed tourists on the upper deck wore headphones and stared straight ahead, as still as mannequins or corpses. Tully waved before he could stop himself, and wondered if the bus had a tour guide, or if the tourists listened to a tape. He wasn't bothered by Frank's rudeness, in part because Frank had always been rude and Tully was used to it, and in part because Tully was grateful that he didn't have to go to Harrisburg. Harrisburg was about forty miles north of Gettysburg, and Tully felt his soul leaning south. Traveling north, even for an hour, would have been unpleasant, like rowing a boat upstream to reach a place he really didn't want to go. Tully was only nine hours from home. He could sense Maryland, West Virginia, and Virginia stretching out beneath him, and beyond that, almost within range of his imagination, was North Carolina. So far Tully had been able to imagine only as far as Fancy Gap, Virginia. He wanted to stay where he was and not give up any ground.

Tully was traveling alone because Crystal was mad at him, and the entire trip, even on the way up, when he drove in the wrong direction, had been a journey back to her. Crystal was angry because Tully had told her, in bed, the night before they were to leave for New Jersey, that in college he had gone out with Monica Mensing, one of Crystal's sorority sisters, while he was going out with Crystal. He and Crystal had been reminiscing about Chapel Hill, and laughing, mainly about Frank, who in college was a man of contradictions. Frank had been a jock, a crew cut, a frat rat and Nixon supporter — who in direct conflict with prevailing fashion wore button-down shirts and creased chinos and penny loafers without socks — but he had also been a closet, if earnest, pothead and an ardent supporter of free love. Frank and Tully had done most of their trolling for girls around the edges of the peace movement, where, somewhat surprisingly, their status as athletes made sex a commodity easy to procure. For some reason Tully thought of Monica Mensing, whom he and Frank had both dated, and from whom Frank had contracted crabs. Tully said, "Hey, Crystal, do you remember Monica Mensing?" and when she stiffened, Tully knew he had made a huge mistake. Crystal's naked leg was draped over his. She moved it. "My God, Tully," she said. "Did you sleep with her?"

For most of their marriage Crystal's anger had been a noise Tully heard from a great distance, and he had been indifferent to it because it seemed so far away. But now it whistled past his ears and seemed to explode inside his stomach and chest, and frightened him in a way he had never been frightened by anything else. Losing Crystal had become Tully's biggest fear — his first old man's fear, he thought — and he dealt with her anger by trying to make whatever caused it right. He didn't understand at first why she was angry about his going out with Monica Mensing — it had happened twenty years ago, at a time when they were still dating other people — and figured it must have something to do with the fact that Monica and Crystal had been sorority sisters. Crystal was an extremely *loyal* person. She still wouldn't show Tully her sorority's secret handshake, and over the years the Chi-Omega handshake had been a point of contention in more than one argument. Thousands of women all over America knew that handshake, and Tully bet that most of them had shown it to their husbands. Of course, he had long ago reached the point where he would have been disappointed if Crystal had relented, and he sometimes caught himself bragging, under the guise of complaint, about Crystal's stubbornness. Tully would touch Crystal with great reverence and contrition when he got home, even though he thought she would probably hate that. He believed Crystal had liked it better in the old days, when he touched her simply because he knew he would get something he wanted.

Eileen was still angry at Frank when she rejoined Tully on the steps, although she tried to pretend she wasn't. Tully recognized in her face an accumulation of small hurts and disappointments he tried to forget ever having seen in Crystal's. For so many years he had been like Frank — not mean, necessarily, just distant and aloof. Tully thought he had been too *tall*. There was so much to make up for, and already he was forty-one years old. Early in their marriage Tully had browbeat Crystal into having a tubal ligation. It had been difficult to find a doctor willing to perform the procedure because Crystal was so young, and young people, the doctors told them, always changed their mind. But Tully had insisted. He had been sure, isolated inside his athlete's solitary arrogance, that he never wanted to share his life with children. Birth control pills made Crystal fat and irritable, and Tully hadn't even been able to imagine *speaking* to a child. He had been wrong, of course — Crystal loved children, and in the last few years even Tully had drawn some suspicious looks in the mall for initiating conversations with small children — and he considered Crystal's tubal ligation an act of selfishness for which he could never atone. He figured the arteries leading from his heart were already partially blocked. He had stopped eating red meat, but he was afraid to mention adoption.

"So, Tully," Eileen said, "what do you do in North Carolina?"

"I sell real estate," Tully said, blushing hard at his cowardice. "And I'm married."

Eileen's eyes widened briefly in surprise, and she laughed. He had accidentally flattered her. "And how was your trip?"

"Fine," Tully said, slightly flattered himself. "Actually, I'm glad it's almost over." Tully as a rule didn't care much for the North. New Jersey had seemed to him a series of warehouses and factories connected by toll roads. All of the real estate seemed commercial or industrial, and he wondered where everybody *lived.* He had forgotten to bring quarters for the toll booths, and the women inside the booths made change contemptuously. Everyone blew their horns a lot. Tully didn't get to speak to Tina until the reception, and then the look on her face told him that she hadn't expected to see him at all, and didn't know why he had come. He realized then he had gone to Tina's wedding out of some misguided, and possibly pathetic, sense of nostalgia. When they were kids, Tully had considered his love for his cousin so tragic that one Thanksgiving he climbed into the loft of his grandparents' barn and thought about becoming an atheist. For that he had driven all the way to New Jersey. At the reception Tina did an exaggerated double take. "Tully?" she said. Tully was simply a name on a list, a *relation.* "God, I never expected to see you here." In his hand Tully clutched a box containing two goblets Crystal had picked out. The fact that the goblets were crystal made Tully's heart ache. He was a long way from home. He handed Tina the box, and immediately wanted it back. Crystal had wrapped it herself. An hour after Tully admitted sleeping with Monica Mensing, after he thought the sins of his past would track him no longer that night, Crystal rolled over and said, "So, tell me, Tully, did you use a *rubber?* Did you have to wait for her *period?*" In New Jersey he felt disengaged and lost in the world. He tried to smile at his cousin. "Here's some goblets," he said.

Eileen and Tully crossed the square on foot, an adventure during which Eileen displayed the righteous belief of a Gettysburg native that the traffic pouring in and out of the square would yield to pedestrians. Tully wasn't so sure, however, and entered the intersections only after the traffic had come to a complete halt. He felt like Frankenstein following the little girl. Once across the square they stopped in front of the Wills House, where Lincoln stayed the night before he delivered the Gettysburg Address. The house was now a museum, in front of which stood a realistic statue of Lincoln explaining something written on a sheet of paper to a statue of a man wearing a pullover sweater and corduroys and running shoes. Lincoln pointed with his hat. "This is so stupid," Eileen said. "Only in Get-

tysburg would they build a statue of a tourist asking
Abraham Lincoln for directions."

Tully had never seen a statue of a tourist before, and
didn't want to believe he was seeing one now. "Maybe
he's asking Lincoln about the Gettysburg Address," he
said. "Don't you think that's it?"

"Nope, this guy wants to know how to get to Land
of Little Horses." Eileen put her hands on her hips and
stepped up close to the statue. "Hey, touron," she said,
"Land of Little Horses is out Route 30. Now beat it and
don't be here when I get back."

The Blue Lagoon, the restaurant and bar to which
they were headed, had a CLOSED sign on the door, but
Eileen led Tully down a long alley off Baltimore Street,
through an unmarked steel door, and down a narrow,
unlit hallway into the kitchen. "The owner locks the
front door on Sundays," Eileen said, "so the locals can
come in and get a beer. It's a secret." They pushed
through a set of saloon doors into the darkened dining
room, which was stark, and cheaply furnished. The
tables were surrounded by mismatched wooden chairs,
and covered with red and white plastic tablecloths. On
each tablecloth an old, wax-covered Chianti bottle
sprouted a red candle. A single fishnet tacked to the
wall, along with a few stray watercolors of the sea, were
the Blue Lagoon's only nautical references. The chan-
delier was made out of an old wagon wheel. Tully was
glad the owner would never appear in his office in North
Carolina and ask him to sell it. It would be hard to
move.

The Blue Lagoon's bar was brighter than the dining room, although the lights were off and the blinds covering the large window facing the street were pulled. Another fishnet hung on the wall, and at a table underneath the net two men a little older than Tully played chess. Tully thought they looked vaguely ethnic and decided they must be native Pennsylvanians. They were fleshy but strong-looking, with dark, thinning hair and prominent, black mustaches. One man nodded without looking up from the chessboard, and the other raised his eyes briefly and called Eileen "Starfish." Neither paid any attention to Tully, not even to how tall he was, which made him feel more welcome than anything else they could have done. He felt local, which was almost as good as being home. Eileen explained that one of the men was Ron, who owned the Blue Lagoon, but made most of his money writing ghost-story books about the battlefield. The other man was Dave, a dentist who discovered a live artillery shell while digging the foundation for his new office. A bored-looking girl stood up behind the bar and Eileen greeted her by holding up two fingers. She led Tully to a table in the back of the bar, where the girl brought each of them a mug of beer. The television set over the bar was tuned to a Baltimore Orioles game, but no one seemed to be watching.

"Why did that guy call you 'Starfish'?"

"That's what I study," Eileen said. "Or what I used to study."

"You don't study them anymore?"

"There are no starfish in Gettysburg, Tully. I've looked."

"I guess not," Tully said. He tried to picture Gettysburg on the map of Pennsylvania in his atlas. He wondered how far it was from the ocean, but all he knew for sure was how far it was from North Carolina.

"Wait. There is one starfish in Gettysburg," Eileen said, pointing to the net on the wall. In the lower-left corner of the net was a small gray star that Tully hadn't noticed before. "That one's mine. The last one. I brought it up here from Florida. They look a lot better alive, actually. That one's dried."

"So what's a marine biologist like you doing in a place like this?"

"I don't know, Tully," she said. "Your guess is as good as mine. Deviant migration pattern, I suppose."

"Deviant migration pattern," Tully said. He liked the way scientific words sounded coming out of his mouth.

"That's right," Eileen said. "The Deviant Migration Pattern of the Midget Systematist."

"You're not a midget," Tully said. He hoped he hadn't spoken up too quickly, or sounded too earnest.

"Technically," Eileen said, "believe it or not, you're actually right. I'm just a very, very *small* systematist."

"Systematist."

"That's right. We describe things. I describe starfish. If you were a systematist and described me as a midget, you would be incorrect. Besides, that's a very ugly word."

"Why starfish?"

"I'm not sure. I guess it's because they look like us, you know? They're this one thing, this very simple animal, but it's like they're trying to be something else."

"They look like us?"

"Yeah, they look like us." Eileen slid out from underneath the table and stood with her feet wide apart, her arms held straight out from her sides. "Look, Tully," she said. "Two arms, two legs, and a head. Five rays. You see?"

"Hey, Starfish," Dave the dentist called out from the front of the bar, "let's hold it down back there. Don't make me get the net."

"Why don't you go home, you big simian?" Eileen called back. "Your kids are in *high school* now, for godsakes. They need a *father*." She sat back down and stared intently at Tully. "You see?"

"Geez," Dave the dentist said. "Did she say *high school*? Somebody should've told me."

"It's true," Ron said. "High school. Your move."

Tully grinned. He felt like Eileen had just given him a present, or directions to a place with a really good view. "I never thought of that before," he said. "Five rays." In the distance Tully could almost make out the world of science.

"Yeah. Five rays. But you see, they're still these simple creatures, echinoderms, which means they have spiny skin. They're related to sea *cucumbers*, that's how simple they are, but they've got these rays. So far they don't show a preference for any particular ray, not the way we show a preference for our heads, but they could, someday, you know? Isn't that something to think about, Tully? I mean, they're *evolving*. That starfish over there is a species called *Luidia clathrata,* which is my baby. Now, there's two types of *Luidia clathrata,* but they're so closely related that they still have the same name, but one type is gray and the other type is tricolored, and there's a few little morphological differences, ossicle arrangement and skeletal structure and stuff, and nobody knows why yet. It could be a speciation event, or it could be environmental, but they're *changing,* you know? They have these different traits. And when you can describe a trait that's uniquely derived, one that's not a shared ancestral trait, then you can distinguish one organism from another organism, and then you've got something. You can get an idea where something is headed. Can you see that? Does that make sense?"

"God," Tully said. "That's great. That's really great. That's what you do?" He felt a little giddy. He was afraid he was going to forget something.

"That's what I do. You don't think it's stupid?"

"No," Tully said. "Of course not. Why would you say that? Does Frank think it's stupid?"

"I don't know what Frank thinks," Eileen said. "But he didn't seem to think that dragging me away from Florida was that big a deal."

"Well, who knows what Frank thinks?" Tully said. He didn't know what else to say.

Eileen traced a star on the side of her beer mug with

her fingernail. "I still need to do about another year's research to finish my dissertation," she said.

"Are you going back to Florida?"

She smiled, but didn't answer immediately. "You're a nice guy, Tully. You really are. I'm going to tell you my favorite thing about starfish."

"OK," Tully said. "I'm ready." He concentrated and hoped it was something he could remember and tell Crystal.

"Here goes. If you cut a ray off of a starfish, as long as there's a little bit of the central disc left, then the starfish will not only grow a new ray, but the *ray* will grow a new starfish."

"No kidding," said Tully.

"Don't tell Frank."

"Why not?"

"I'm afraid he would try it."

After they left the Blue Lagoon, Eileen took Tully to a miniature Gothic castle built at the summit of Little Round Top, one of the two hills that overlooked the southern end of the battlefield. Plaques identified it as a monument honoring troops from the Forty-fourth New York. Tully remembered that Confederate forces almost overran Little Round Top on the second day of the battle, which would have given victory to the South. A desperate bayonet charge by a Maine regiment had perhaps saved the Union. Tully was pleased that he was finally beginning to connect his reading with the places he saw.

Eileen had produced a map of the battlefield from the glove compartment of her car, and during the drive along Confederate Avenue Tully was able to figure out for himself how the lines of the two armies had been positioned. When they passed the area from which General Pickett launched his famous charge, Tully looked across the grassy fields and located the little clump of trees at which the attack had been aimed. The trees had marked the center of the Union line, and were exactly where Tully expected them to be, which made him feel less stupid than he had at any time since telling Crystal about Monica Mensing. He remembered that the spot where the charge briefly broke through, before being beaten back, was known as the High Water Mark of the Confederacy, but Tully refrained from mentioning it to Eileen. She seemed to know exactly where she was going. Frank would be the one who had never bothered to tour the battlefield. Frank never went to the beach in Florida.

Inside the monument a rope tied between two orange barrels sealed off the entrance to the staircase inside the turret. Tully turned to leave, but Eileen held her finger to her lips and motioned for Tully to follow. She ducked beneath the rope and disappeared up the stairs. Tully looked around to see if anyone was watching and then stepped over the rope. The spiral staircase was narrow, barely wide enough for Tully's shoulders. Small hollows had been worn over the years into the stone stairs until they were no longer flat. They were smooth to the point of slickness. Tully assumed the stairway was closed because someone had fallen. He climbed the steps slightly stooped, holding on to the granite wall with one hand and the gleaming bronze handrail with the other, afraid that he was going to slip, or bump his head on some low overhang. He marveled again at how tiny Eileen was, and noted that the monument seemed to have been built to her scale. She looked perfectly normal climbing the cramped stairs, while Tully experienced the uncomfortable sensation of having grown even bigger — to the point where buildings, even castles, no longer fit — which made the staircase seem even more narrow and forbidding. He was glad when they finally stepped through a doorway onto a small terrace surrounded by low battlements.

The most famous battlefield in American history spread out beneath Little Round Top, and as Tully looked up the gut of the valley toward Gettysburg, across the lush fields and woods, he prepared himself to experience some type of revelation, a moment when some ancestral voice inside him would say, "*Here. This is the place.*" But what he felt was absolutely nothing, save a real estate broker's generic appreciation of the view. "*Here. Condos here would be big.*" Tully felt his grandmother's stories about the battle growing smaller and smaller inside him. There was nothing in the valley to suggest that a great battle had ever been fought there, that one hundred and seventy-two thousand men had for three days rushed at one another in anger, that history had met in a point beneath him, before moving off in directions the men who fought there could not have imagined. Gettysburg, Tully realized, the only Gettysburg he could know, was simply a small town surrounded by a park.

An almost constant stream of traffic moved slowly along the roads that circled the battlefield, and at the bottom of the hill to Tully's left a platoon of tourists swarmed over Devil's Den, the rock formation that had been the site of some of the battle's most bitter fighting. They were pointing and shouting things Tully couldn't hear and posing for photographs. They were on *vacation*. Until that moment Tully had harbored a secret hope that he might find some evidence of the battle to take home — a minié ball, a shell fragment, a small piece of bone — but realized that the ground had been picked clean. The scent of history was cold. One of the reasons Tully had always loved his grandmother's stories about the war was that she clearly remembered her grandfather William, who became a preacher upon returning from the war, primarily because his wounded arm was useless and he could no longer farm. His grandmother's childhood memory of an old man with a crooked arm had always allowed Tully to say that he knew someone who had known someone who had fought in the Civil War. Over a hundred years of history disappeared every time he said that. But now, on Little Round Top, Tully could find nothing in the landscape to suggest that anyone with his blood had ever been there before, or would ever be back. Uncle John had disappeared all over again.

"What are you thinking about?" Eileen said.

"I'm thinking that it doesn't seem like anybody ever got in a fight here."

"Except me and Frank. We fight here all the time."

"Except you and Frank. Can you see your house from here?"

Eileen shielded her eyes with her hand and gazed into the distance. "Nope," she said. "Maybe in the winter. I don't know. Not now. It's over there somewhere." She waved her hand in the general direction of town, and looked up at Tully and smiled expectantly. Tully could tell she wanted to talk about Frank. He wished there were something on the terrace to sit on. Eileen was a lot easier to talk to when they were sitting down. Tully was afraid to sit on one of the battlements, because he might fall off.

"So what are you and Frank fighting about?"

"Oh, a lot of things," Eileen said. "Pennsylvania. Starfish. The fact that I forget to slide the seat in the Saab back after I drive it. You know. Stuff like that."

"Wow," Tully said. "Frank lets you drive the Saab?"

Eileen laughed. "Sometimes. If I've been real good, and haven't said anything stupid lately. Frank thinks I'm too stupid to even *drive*."

"You're not stupid."

"I know that. I just say stupid stuff to piss Frank off. Sometimes you have to say stupid stuff to get the big jerk to even *speak*, and then he says, 'God, Eileen. That was so stupid. Why do you say stupid things like that,

Eileen?' and then I say, 'Why do you always call me stupid? I'm not stupid. You're stupid, you big jerk,' and then we get in a fight, and then after we yell a lot I can make him tell me that he loves me, which really pisses him off."

"Frank hates to lose."

"I know. I especially like fighting during ball games," Eileen said. "Frank really hates it when I talk during ball games, so it doesn't take nearly as long to make him mad." She grinned slyly. "So tell me, Tully, why is your wife mad at you?"

Tully tried to think of something funny to say, but the truth crawled up from inside him and out his mouth into the sun before he could stop it. "My wife is mad at me because a long time ago I made her get her tubes tied, and now both of us wish we could've had babies. That's the short version." For a moment his heart fluttered like a small animal, and he thought he was going to hyperventilate. He did not want to die in Pennsylvania.

"Oh no," Eileen said. "I am so sorry, Tully. I didn't mean to make you tell me that. That was a secret. I didn't know you were going to tell me a secret."

"That's OK," he said. "Neither did I." Tully looked away from Eileen and tried to find the Peach Orchard in the valley beneath them. Something important had happened in the Peach Orchard on the second day.

"Do you want me to tell you a secret?"

"Only if you want to," Tully said. "You don't have

to." Tully really didn't want to hear a secret weighty enough to match his.

"OK, here goes," Eileen said. "Frank gave me herpes." She grinned brightly, almost as if she were proud, and then swallowed and bit her lip, waiting to see what Tully would say. He wondered if he was the first person she had told.

"Jesus, Eileen," he said. "That was a big secret."

"That's what we're fighting about," said Eileen. "I'm having an outbreak. Every time one of us has an outbreak Frank feels so bad and guilty about giving it to me he can't even talk. So we always end up fighting. He feels like he did this terrible thing to me."

"Well, God, Eileen," Tully said. "He did. He gave you *herpes*."

"I know, but he says he didn't know he had it when he gave it to me, and I just have to believe that. Sometimes you just have to believe something before you can do anything else, you know? And it's awful, sure. God, I'm not like a herpes *person* or anything, but it's not something that I have to think about every single day of my life. Some days I don't even think about it at all. Of course, this isn't one of those days."

"I'm really sorry, Eileen," he said. "Frank should have been more careful. That was really stupid."

"It's OK, Tully. Not really, you know, there's no cure, but the way I kind of look at it is that whenever I have an outbreak, and I have to go to the gynecologist, and then I have to go to the drugstore, and I have to use all this *medicine*, then I have to think about Frank, you know? I can't help but thinking about Frank. It was going to be tough for me to have kids anyway, and now it might be really tough. And whenever Frank has it, then he has to think about me, because he gave it to me, and it changed my life as much as it changed his. It makes us think about each other, and it will always make us think about each other, whether we stay together or not. I could go back to Florida and stay forever, but I would still have to think about Frank, and Frank would still have to think about me. Does that make sense? I mean, does that sound really stupid?"

Tully shook his head no with what he hoped was enough conviction.

"Frank says it's really stupid. He doesn't like to talk about it at all, but I think it's kind of like these saints they used to make us read about in school. These saints, they lived a long time ago, used to whip themselves with branches, and wear belts made out of thorns because it made them think about God."

"I don't know, Eileen," Tully said. "I don't know if I could think about things like that. I don't like to think about what I did to Crystal."

"But doesn't what you did to her make you think about how much you love her?"

"Well, yeah. But I'd rather think about that without having to think about Crystal getting her tubes tied. That was the worst thing I ever did in my life. I don't want to think about that all the time."

Eileen climbed up on one of the battlements and

looked Tully in the eye. Tully wondered if he could grab her in time if she started to fall. It was a long way to the ground. "But *would* you think about her, Tully? Would you really? If there weren't bad things in the world, then we wouldn't know there were good things. Everything would be the same, and we wouldn't even know. We might as well be invertebrates."

"Invertebrates," Tully said.

"Actually, forget I said that. That's a pretty arbitrary and homocentric way to classify animals. Things like us and things not like us. That's not good science."

Tully felt as if he were losing a race with Eileen. He felt dumb, and he felt old. "Eileen," he said, "what in the world are you doing with Frank?"

Eileen giggled and hopped down off of the battlement. "God, Tully. Frank is just so *radial,* you know? The first time I ever saw him, he was in this student bar in one of his development-office suits, with this big, painted bimbo woman, and I thought, 'Wow, that's really a radial guy.' But, what you have to realize about Frank is that he's trying to be *bilateral.* Frank's this big, stupid, primitive organism, but he's trying to grow this extra chamber in his heart. It's so amazing to watch. This morning he tried to save those baby birds, which was so sweet, but the way he did it was so incredibly stupid that you just want to measure his *brain.* But then he felt so bad about leaving them out in the sun that he yelled at me, like I had something to do with it. Then he takes them all the way to Harrisburg in his brand-new Saab, when he won't even let me eat a potato chip in it, and the birds are probably going to die anyway. Personally, I would've given them to a *cat*. I mean, I love Frank, I just don't know how to *classify* him."

Tully and Eileen heard the chimney swifts inside the house when they walked up on the porch. When Eileen opened the front door they found Frank, again clad in the yellow gloves, trying to coax one of the birds into attaching itself to a towel he had wrapped around the end of a broom. The broom leaned against the mantel over the fireplace. One of the birds already clung to the towel with both claws, upside down, but squawked as if it were afraid of falling. The bird Frank held squawked in unison. Frank looked up and grinned. "Hey, you two," he said. "There you are. Where you been? Having an affair?"

"You caught us," Eileen said. "We would've been back sooner, but Tully likes to cuddle after he's finished."

"Tully," Frank said. "You are so sweet."

"Thanks. What are you doing?"

"I'm going to shove these little guys back up the chimney, which is what I should've done in the first place."

"I thought you were going to leave them in Harrisburg," Eileen said. "With PAW."

"Nah," said Frank, "PAW said they would take them, but they would probably die. The woman I talked to said their best shot was to put them back up the chimney."

"They could've told you that on the phone."

"This was a different woman than the one I talked to the first time. This woman was really sharp. She's a vet. We mashed up some worms and fed these guys. God, were they hungry. You wouldn't believe how much they ate." Frank held one of his hands below the second bird, to catch it if it fell, and then tentatively removed his other hand. The bird looked more like something Frank had smeared onto the towel than it did a bird. It didn't let go, although it bleated out what Tully figured must be the chimney-swift equivalent of a scream. "Hey, look at that," Frank said. "Way to hang, guys. Look at those claws. What do you think, Tully? Are these some great birds or what?"

"They're great birds," Tully said.

"Boy are they going to have some stories to tell," Frank said. "They're like a day old, and already they fell down a chimney and got stuck out in the sun and rode in a car and went all the way to Harrisburg. How many chimney sweeps can say that?"

"Not many, probably," Tully said.

"Damn right," said Frank. "But these are some tough birds. I named them Butkus and Singletary."

"Butkus and Singletary?" Eileen said.

"Yeah. Tough guys. When they grow up, and start flying around outside, they'll kick some blue-jay ass. Cats will be afraid of these guys."

Eileen moved closer and studied the two swifts. They had stopped squawking, and had settled down into sort of a periodic concerned chirping. "They look better," she said. "You did a good job. Now you're going to stick that broom up the chimney?"

"That's the plan." Frank had stacked three cement blocks in the fireplace, on which to prop the broom, so that the birds would be as high up as possible.

"And the doctor thinks that the mama bird will come back and feed them?"

"She says maybe. And if she don't, then it's you and me, kid. We're their daddy and mama. Tully, you can be their uncle."

"I was afraid of this," Eileen said. "My children are named Butkus and Singletary."

Frank squatted down and gingerly lifted the broom. Eileen cupped her hands beneath the birds in case one of them let go of the towel. Frank maneuvered the broom into the fireplace and then up through the damper until he was able to place the end of the handle on the cement blocks. "There you go, boys," he said. "Make a lot of noise so mama will know you're home."

Eileen leaned into the fireplace and tried to look up the chimney. "I wouldn't do that if I were you, baby," Frank said. "The boys had a big lunch."

Tully and Frank stood in Frank's front yard in the twilight and watched swifts wheel in and out of the chimney. "It's amazing how many birds there are in there," Frank said. "I'll bet there's fifty or more. Somebody's bound to be taking care of the boys. Don't you think so?"

"Yeah, I do, Frank," Tully said. He wasn't sure if he believed it or not, but he wanted to be reassuring. "That many birds aren't going to let two little guys starve."

"Chimney sweeps are so funny looking," Frank said. "They've got pointed wings and they don't fly straight. They look kind of like bats."

Tully tried, but could not follow the flight of a particular bird for very long. They did look like bats.

"I guess it's so they can chase insects," Frank said. "That's probably why their wings are shaped like that."

"Frank, you just described a bird."

"I know," said Frank. "It worries me."

"I think it's sweet."

Frank shook his head. "I've got to get that girl to some starfish, Tully. She's driving me crazy, always worrying about starfish. I could've lived my whole life and never thought once about starfish. Now I know their damn names."

"*Luidia clathrata*," Tully said. He'd had Eileen write the name down in his atlas.

"See?" Frank said. "Look at us, Tully. We know the scientific name of a freaking starfish. Can you believe that?"

"Eileen's really smart, you know," Tully said.

"I know that," said Frank.

"I mean, she's really smart."

"I *know* that, Tully. She's really, really smart."

"I really like her."

"Well I like her, too," said Frank.

"So what are you going to do?"

"What do you mean, 'What am I going to do?'"

"I mean, what are you going to do?"

"Look, Tully," Frank said. "I'm living with Eileen, right?"

"Yeah," Tully said. "So?"

"So in all the years you've known me, have I ever lived with anybody before?"

Tully thought for a second. "No. I guess not. You've never lived with anybody before."

"All right, then," said Frank. "There you go."

The next morning after breakfast Tully and Eileen and Frank knelt by the fireplace and listened until they decided that the various flutterings and chirps coming from the chimney were the result of the two baby swifts' mother feeding them breakfast. A few minutes later Frank said, "Tully, don't take any wooden nickels," and left for work in the Saab. Tully and Eileen laughed after Frank left because the college was only two blocks away. Tully laughed uneasily because he and Crystal had recently started recycling. He carried his bag to the car and returned to the porch to say good-bye to Eileen. She climbed onto a chair and held out her arms, and when Tully stepped close she kissed him on the cheek with a loud smack. "Don't worry, Tully," she said. "I don't have it on my mouth." She presented Tully with a pair of starfish earrings to give to Crystal. Tully told her Crystal would love them, at the same time knowing a pair of small, gold hoops were the only earrings Crystal ever wore. The first tour bus of the day rolled up Lincoln Avenue, and it was still chilly enough out that the tourists on the top deck wore sweaters. "Tourons," Eileen said. "Everybody wants to see something." Tully kissed Eileen lightly on the lips. "Bye, Luidia," he said. She was still standing on the chair when Tully turned off of Lincoln Avenue onto Carlisle and could no longer see her in his mirror. He drove through town to the park's visitor center, where he bought a biography of Stonewall Jackson and two copies of the Gettysburg Confederate death roster, in which he had been surprised, and more than a little disappointed, to find the entry **John Parker Womack Cpl., Co. C, 55th North Carolina.** Of all the artifacts from the battle Tully studied in the museum, the thing he would remember most was a small knife a Union soldier used to amputate his own leg after it was struck by a Confederate artillery shell. The card beneath the knife said that the soldier cheerfully completed the operation, but died a few minutes later. On his way out of the museum, Tully called his wife from a pay phone in the lobby. Crystal did not say that she loved him or that she had missed him, but when she told him to drive carefully, he considered it enough. He stepped into the sun squinting and larval and soft. He carried his new books under his arm. He thought about a wounded soldier growing a new leg, and a wounded leg growing a new soldier. He thought about the two soldiers marching home, and wondered if they would know the same things when they got there. He had only a dim imagining of the place he wanted to go, and only the most basic notion about how to get there. He drove southwest for almost seven hours, and from the top of the mountain at Fancy Gap, Virginia, thought he could almost see it.

LORD RANDALL

MY MOTHER named me Randall after Lord Randall, this guy whose true love kills him by getting him to eat some poisoned eels. She won a talent show in high school playing the mandolin and singing Lord Randall's song. She doesn't seem to think any bad could come from naming a baby after somebody whose luck was that awful, but I'm not so sure. I drove a school bus for a little while when I was in high school, and one morning a first grader named John Fitzgerald Kennedy Canipe ran right out in front of me. I would've run over him if I hadn't been watching out for him especially, the way I always did, once I found out what his name was. I realize you can say that Jeff-Kay Canipe's name brought him good luck just as easily as you can say that it brought him bad luck, but what it proves to me is that the world is crazy with all kinds of luck and you can't be too careful. I quit driving the school bus.

Now Jeff-Kay Canipe pumps gas at the Municipal Marina, and I see him there on the dock whenever I go past, on the way up to my parents' place. He is famous among kids in these parts because he can spin just about anything on his finger — gas cans, ski vests, tackle boxes, coolers — and make it look like everybody ought to be able to do it. He does it without even realizing he's doing it, the way someone else might twist their hair or chew on their lip. He will stand and talk to you with a boat paddle spinning slowly on his finger, and never even look up at it. It will drive you crazy, waiting for it to fall. He doesn't remember that I drove his school bus the year he started to school, and doesn't know that I'm responsible for everything that has happened to him, good and bad, since 1973.

When I go see my parents, my mother throws open the door of their trailer and clasps her hands to her chest like she's dying and sings out in a high, quavery voice, "Oh, where have you been, Lord Randall my son? Oh, where have you been, my handsome young man?" which even after all these years still makes me nervous. If I say anything at all, I say, "I've been down the mountain because that's where I live." That satisfies her, but what she really wants me to do is sing, "I'm wearied with hunting, and fain would lie down," the way I did when I was a little kid. Back then she played her mandolin and sang the first part of the verses, and I sang the second part, and she showed me off to anybody who would stand still and listen. We had a regular act going until I got a little older and figured out just what exactly had happened to Lord Randall, and how there was no telling what kind of bad luck singing that song out loud

over and over to complete strangers could bring down
on my head.

My mother told me not too long ago that she seriously considered naming me Fain, because fain means
happy and pleased, but that at the time she thought it
sounded too much like Fabian, who had a song out she
didn't like. I owe Fabian a big one. It's my gut feeling
that no good could ever come from being named Fain,
no matter what it means, although you can never say
something like that for sure. Jeff-Kay Canipe could run
a whole school bus full of kids off the side of a mountain
on his way to work in the morning, and one of those
kids could've been the one who grew up and figured out
how to cure cancer. It might turn out that running over
Jeff-Kay Canipe might've been the best thing I could
have done with my life. It might've been the only thing
I was *meant* to do, and I screwed everything up. Jeff-
Kay Canipe has become friends with my parents, and
spends more time at their place than I do. His whole life
is something to consider, and considering it makes me
tired. There's no way of knowing, not yet, how any of
it is going to turn out. All I can say, at the end of the
day, is how it *didn't* turn out. In the meantime, I
wouldn't eat an eel for a million dollars, and I'm fussy
about shrimp and mayonnaise. I won't answer to Randall if I can help it, and Randy almost never. You meet
more assholes who are named Randy than you do with
any other name. My father gave me Lake for a middle
name because we lived close to one, and that is the
name I go by. Our last name is Tesseneer, but I don't

have any idea where it came from or what in the world it means.

My parents are Bonnie and Bud Tesseneer, and they own a trout pond about the size of a good mudhole up above the Girl Scout camp. It's three miles off the main highway, and six miles from the lake, too far out and too small to ever do any good, although they'll tell you, and swear on it, that they're sitting on a gold mine up there, and it's just a matter of time until word gets out and business takes off. They say that any day they'll be covered up with tourists tired of the beaten path worn around the lake, and hungry for fresh mountain trout. I think, *Don't hold your breath,* but don't ever say it out loud. My parents are past the point where knowing anything that resembles the truth would do them any good. They act like little kids running a bait stand, like they're going to make a million dollars selling worms. You have to look out for people like that.

The two of them have always thought they were going to strike it big, and live out their lives rich as royalty, and they've tried to do it a hundred different ways, none of them any more successful than any of the others. Over the years they've run motels and Laundromats and campgrounds, and bait shops and ice-cream parlors and package stores, and service stations and gift shops and boat-rental places, and until the trout pond, always for other people. Every time they got started on something new, they called me up and said, "Lake, this is the break we've been looking for. This is the one, son," but

I could always tell, even on the phone, that they were already planning their next project, the *big* one, the one they've waited and waited and waited on. About five years ago, they got stuck with cases and cases of Amway products they couldn't sell, and they're still not sure how they did it. They just look at each other and giggle when you ask about it. Every time I go up there they try to give me a bagful. They never get tired of making jokes about suede cleaner. Sometimes I think that when they look at the trout pond, they can't even see it, not really. Sometimes I look at it and try to imagine what they see, but what it always looks like to me is trouble. My parents are both over sixty and can't keep their hands off each other and don't have any insurance and worry the hell out of me.

For four or five years when I was a kid, they were caretakers at a summer camp for boys down on the lake. It was the thing they did longer than anything else. I liked living there a lot in the winter, when all the city kids weren't there, and almost every night I'd take the camp master key and a pile of quilts so big I couldn't hardly carry it, and go down and sleep in one of the cabins. A lot of nights my mother and father made a lot of noise in their room, and after I got old enough to know what it was, I didn't want to listen to it. I guess there were thirty or more cabins in the camp, all close enough to the lake that you could hear the water running up on the shore when the wind blew it, and every one felt different than all the others when you lay in it at night. I always told my parents which cabin I was going to sleep in, so they could find me in the morning, but sometimes they'd forget to come wake me up, and I'd miss the school bus and get in trouble at school the next day. I'd wake up and the sun would be full out. I'd grab up all my quilts and run back to the house, and my parents would be sitting at the kitchen table, drinking coffee, and my father would be drawing a diagram on a napkin with a pen. Whenever they looked up, I could tell by their faces they'd been making one of their big plans and had forgot all about me, so after a while I started taking their alarm clock with me out to the cabins at night, and they never seemed to notice it was gone.

I didn't like the camp that much in the summer because I didn't get to sleep in the cabins anymore, and because I had to spend a lot of my time hiding out in the woods. For some reason, the favorite game at that camp was chasing Lake Tesseneer, and in the free hour the campers got after breakfast, lunch, and supper, a gang of them would gather up and come sneaking around our place, looking for me. If they ever caught me outside, away from the house, they'd cut me off and I'd have to run and hide in the laurel above the lake, and try to circle back and get inside, until the counselors came at the end of the free hour and blew their whistles and called them off. I wasn't really afraid of any of those kids — not one at a time, anyway — and sometimes when I got bored or felt like playing I'd go down to the cabins just as they finished eating to let them get a look at me. All they had to do was just spot me, just catch a *glimpse* of me, and they'd start waving their arms in the air and yelling like they were crazy and light out after me. It was the damndest thing you ever saw. Sometimes I'd run straight up the side of the mountain, and after the gang got spread out in a long line behind me, I'd turn around and circle back and tear down the side of the mountain at full speed, and jump out of the laurel and holler and scare the hell out of the little kids and the slow kids who ran at the tail end of the line and weren't too keen on catching me anyway. There was never any question of them running me down, not even the new big fast kid who came every summer and was supposed to be able to catch me singlehanded once and for all. They were just a bunch of city kids from Charleston and Savannah and Atlanta who couldn't find their butts in the woods, but by the end of the summer hiding and running and being *wary* all the time would start to get old. I'd get mad and go down to the cabins late at night and throw big rocks from the campfire pits onto the tin roofs, just to make all the city kids inside whisper, "What was that?" and root around in the dark for their flashlights. After a minute every flashlight in the place would come on, and the beams would shoot out through the screens, and the counselors would yell, "Shut Up!" and "Turn Off Those Lights!" and come to the door of the cabin in their underwear and open it and look around, as if they would be able to see me. If I was real lucky, they would be pissed off and yell out my name, which always made me feel good, hiding out in the dark and watching. It made the city kids howl out loud and swear that they would get me the next day and thrash around and take forever getting back to sleep.

The only big days my parents ever have at the trout pond come once or twice a summer when a troop of Girl Scouts rides up the hill in a big red school bus to fish. My parents look forward to them coming all winter, but I think it's one of the scariest things I've ever seen. The little girls stand shoulder to shoulder all the way around the pond and jerk trout out of the water as fast as the counselors can put corn on their hooks. They dance around and around and squeal when they catch one, and get their lines tangled up in the lines around them, most of which also have a trout thrashing on the other end. You can hear the ruckus for miles. I watch the whole thing from the kitchen window of my parents' trailer, through a crack in the curtains. That many kids that age all together are just poked-out eyes and bad accidents waiting to happen. From a distance it looks like the fish are jumping up out of the water and dodging around in the air, trying to fight their way out of the pond and make a break for the higher mountains where the real trout live, but the Girl Scouts are beating them back down into the water with long sticks.

The scouts always have a big fish fry down at the camp the night after they fish, and invite my parents. I went once and won't ever go back. All those little girls sat cross-legged in a circle around a big campfire, gnawing on trout, not even looking for bones, and my mother stood by the fire, even though it was a hot night, and played her mandolin and sang. She knows more songs than anybody I know, but in almost all of them somebody gets shot or hung or stabbed or poisoned because of a misunderstanding and dies with their true love's name on their lips. I say, "Mama, don't you know any happy songs?" and she says, "Lake, what could be happier than a song about Love?" My mother says about love what she says about everything else, that it's all in the way you look at it.

Once when I was a little boy I caught a bunch of lightning bugs and put them in a green bottle and put the bottle on the table beside my bed. My mother came in and told me how pretty my lightning bugs were, and then sat there and told me a sad story about how lightning bugs were lost souls flying around in the darkness trying to find their way to heaven. After that all I could think about was all the souls that would never make it because I'd suffocated them first in a 7-Up bottle. That night at the Girl Scout camp, after she sang four or five songs and got good and sad, she walked over and stood directly in front of me and sang "Lord Randall" like her heart would break. She even teared up when she got to the part where the mother tells Lord Randall that the eels were bad and he is poisoned. My father looked up at her like she was an angel, like he had never heard the song before, and had no idea she could even sing. He rocked back and forth and clapped his hands together, not even in time to the music. I could tell that all those little girls were studying us while they ate, and could figure out our whole lives just from watching. I couldn't see their eyes in the firelight, only black holes where their eyes were supposed to be. I could hear them chew. It made the short hairs stand up on the back of my neck, and I put down my plate and stopped eating. I figured that if I was ever going to get a fish bone stuck in my throat and flop around on the ground and die gasping for air, it would be right then, with my mother singing "Lord Randall" and crying and my father clapping and those wild little girls gathered around watching with trout skeletons in their hands.

I work in town down the mountain, where I am a janitor. I do not see anything wrong with this. I have plenty of insurance, medical and life. I play basketball on a team in the city league, because I believe that you start to get old the day you forget how to run. Running is the biggest thing little kids can do that old people can't. I'm thirty-four, and I make sure I do my share. Jeff-Kay Canipe, who is a basketball wizard, is on my team. He's very short, but he can spin basketballs on the middle finger of both hands at the same time until you get tired of watching. He can throw long passes behind his back at a dead run and hit teammates in the head who you would swear he had never looked at. He can see things we can't. Sometimes three or four guys on the other team will surround Jeff-Kay Canipe and try to hem him in and take the ball away, but he dribbles behind his back and through his legs and always gets away clean. My parents come to all of our games, which sometimes makes him show off. I personally am not

very good. The boys in the city league call me The Lake
Monster, I guess because they like the way it sounds
when they say it, and because when I play I wear cutoff
jeans and black high-top sneakers I found in a dumpster.
There was nothing wrong with the shoes that a good
washing didn't fix, and they were my size. They call Jeff-
Kay Canipe Special K. He actually gave $150 for his
shoes, and he won't even wear them outside.

Whenever I get on the floor — which is never more
than four or five minutes a half — the other players roll
their eyes and smile and tell the guy who guards me to
look out for The Lake Monster. That I'm dangerous. I
pretend I don't notice. When we have the ball, I run hard
as I can in a big circle that goes from near midcourt to
underneath the basket and back out again. After a while
the man on the other team gets tired of running around
in a big circle with me. Then he starts saying "Jesus,
Lake, where the hell are you going?" and shrugging and
rolling his eyes every time he runs by his friends in the
bleachers or one of the guys on his team, and just lets
me go. That's my plan. When that happens, I just keep
running in my big circle like I didn't notice, but I keep
my eye on Jeff-Kay Canipe, who I never see looking at
me, but know that he is. At least once a game he throws
me the ball while I'm running close to the basket and all
I have to do is toss it in. This may not sound like much
of an accomplishment to you, but I don't know how to
play basketball. After I score a basket, while we run
back down the court, Jeff-Kay Canipe slaps me on the

butt and looks up and says, "Keep your eye on me, buddy. I'll take good care of you." He looks like he's going to float out of the gym, he's so happy.

I never know what my parents are going to do next. Earlier this summer at the flea market in Asheville they bought a miniature stagecoach and two ponies to pull it. I thought, *A stagecoach*. The ponies are named Roy and Dale, and my father said that the whole rig was a steal at $850. On Sundays he and my mother go down to the lake and take little kids on stagecoach rides, in a circle out the point from the Community Center to the Municipal Marina and back again. The stagecoach holds two kids at a time, sitting knee to knee, and my parents charge two bucks a kid. The ride takes fifteen minutes. Jeff-Kay Canipe steps out and waves from the Municipal Marina when my father turns the stagecoach around. Sometimes he will spin something on his finger — a boat paddle, a broomstick, a fire extinguisher — and the kids will hang out the windows of the stagecoach and look back backward all the way to the Community Center. For another two bucks my mother will take a Polaroid picture of a kid standing with my father and Roy and Dale, or just with Roy and Dale, if they prefer. My parents think they're going to pay off the stagecoach this summer, but I'm not so sure.

The stagecoach is painted bright red, and my mother painted THE B B STAGECOACH LINE, LTD. on the side of it in fancy gold letters. On the back it says THINK

TROUT! My father wears blue jeans and cowboy boots and a red western shirt and two toy pistols, and my mother wears a long red old-fashioned dress and a big red-checked sunbonnet that she ties up in a big bow under her chin. Sometimes she rides up on the seat beside my father with her arm hooked through his, but usually she stays behind and talks to the parents. She keeps her mandolin and several jars of the preserves she makes and the honey my father gathers from the hives behind their trailer and flyers advertising the trout pond and circular-saw blades that she paints mountain scenes on and an assortment of Amway products all arranged on a red cloth on the hood of their truck. If one of the parents points at the mandolin and says, "Can you play that?" my mother will say, "Oh, just a little bit." Then she picks it up and plays it like crazy and closes her eyes and sings one of her sad songs. The parents usually buy something then. Whenever my father climbs up on the seat, he snaps the reins and tilts his head a little back toward the windows and says, "Yee-Hah. I Hope We Don't See Any Indians On This Trip." My mother clasps her hands together and looks up at him like he was the grandest thing she ever saw. The little kids in the back roll their eyes.

My mother and father are able to chain their stage-coach to the willow tree behind the Community Center during the week, free of charge, but they have to keep Roy and Dale at home. They don't have a horse trailer to haul the ponies back and forth, though they say

they're going to buy one as soon as business picks up. Roy is a liver and white pinto gelding, and Dale is a palomino mare. Dale's eyes are blue, if you look at them right, and she's pretty, like a toy. Dale won't let me get within ten feet of her, and I don't know what her problem is. My mother says it's my worldview. On Sundays my father walks the ponies the six miles to the lake, and then the six miles home again at the end of the day. He has angina, and keeps nitroglycerin pills in the pocket of his shirt. My parents never mention it, and look at me like I'm not speaking English whenever I ask. My mother drives the truck a little bit ahead of my father and the ponies and parks where the shoulder of the road is wide enough. She watches in the rearview mirror as they walk toward her. She lets them catch her and go on past out of sight, and then she starts the truck and catches and passes them again, and drives on to the next wide spot on the side of the road. She carries a jug of water for my father, and sugar cubes for Roy and Dale. It takes them two and a half, sometimes three hours to make the trip, going and coming. They leave for the lake before dawn and get home in the pitch dark. Half of the trip is on the state highway, and sometimes assholes pulling big ski boats behind their new trucks blow their horns or throw things out the window or lean out and yell, trying to scare the ponies, which isn't hard to do. Dale is nervous anyway. The cars go by close enough to touch, and the traffic is bad on Sundays with skiers going to the lake and tourists going beyond the lake to the mountains. I'm afraid that one day Dale's going to run out into the highway in front of a bus and drag my father and Roy with her. That my mother will see the whole thing. Sometimes I wake up real early on Sunday mornings and lie in bed and wonder where my parents are on the road to the lake, and just what in the world they're thinking.

Two or three times a day on Sunday my mother has to take her display of stuff off the hood of their truck and drive home to put gasoline in the portable generator that runs the aerator for the pond. Without the aerator pumping oxygen into the water, the trout would die in a couple of hours, all five thousand of them, and I have no idea what my parents would do then. The generator holds only enough gas to run four hours at a time, but it doesn't seem to make them nervous. My father gets up at two o'clock in the morning, and again at six to put gas in it. He does it seven nights a week. Sometimes my mother gets up with him and makes a pot of coffee and they sit in lawn chairs close together on the far side of the pond and talk all night. My mother says it's peaceful, but I don't see how. The generator is loud, and it's a fact of my parents' lives, the awful noise it makes. When you leave their place, after you've been there a while, you always think you've left something, or forgot to do something important, but you can't remember what it is, all because the noise is gone from inside your head.

My parents buy all the gas they use from Jeff-Kay Canipe at the Municipal Marina. Jeff-Kay Canipe always asks how the trout are doing, as if he knew them personally, and on Sundays, if business is slow at the marina, he walks out the road to the Community Center to talk to my parents and pet the ponies. They bring an extra lawn chair so that he will have a place to sit when he visits. Once a tourist asked if he was their son. My parents tell him stories about how well I got along with the city boys at the summer camp, about how we spent our summers whooping and hollering and running through the woods. My mother has taken to calling Jeff-Kay Canipe my little brother, although she knows it makes me mad.

Jeff-Kay Canipe is especially fond of Dale, and Dale likes Jeff-Kay Canipe, which doesn't do a lot for my disposition, either. Dale has a deep sore on the inside of her right front leg that won't heal, and after Jeff-Kay Canipe gets off work in the evenings he comes up to the pond and helps my father put purple medicine on Dale's sore, and motor oil around it to keep the flies away. After they put the medicine on Dale's leg, she runs around the pasture kicking and bucking and biting at the air and making a noise deep in her chest like fighting and won't let my father get near her for a long time. In a few minutes, though, she'll come right up to Jeff-Kay Canipe and butt her head against his arm. Jeff-Kay Canipe gives her sugar cubes and brushes out her mane and whispers in her ear. My mother asks him what he said, but he says it's a secret between him and Dale. She says to me, when Jeff-Kay Canipe isn't listening, "Lake, your little brother sure is good with animals," and I think, *Well, maybe I could've just bumped him a little bit.*

Unlike Dale, Roy will let me pet him, but doesn't seem to care much about it one way or another. He's even-tempered and indifferent to everything except Dale. My mother says that Roy is in love with Dale, but that their relationship was doomed from the beginning because Roy is a gelding, which keeps Dale from loving him back. Whenever Dale runs wild around the pasture, trying to buck the burning place off her leg, Roy trots along behind her, stiff-legged, with his ears up straight, blowing out through his nostrils. My mother says Roy is asking Dale if she is all right. Sometimes, either early in the morning or late in the afternoon, just before dusk, Dale lets Roy mount her. Roy doesn't do anything — there's not much he can do — he just stands there until Dale turns around and looks at him like she just noticed him for the first time, and bucks him off and trots away. My father learned a long time ago to catch Dale first on Sunday mornings. If he led Roy away and never brought him back, Dale would be content to stay by herself in the pasture cropping at the grass, but if my father catches Dale and leads her toward the gate, Roy gets upset and follows Dale as closely as he can. My mother says that Roy wouldn't want to live without Dale, and that if she could make *one* wish, she would wish that Roy could be a stallion for a day. My father says that if it wasn't for the traffic on the highway, he wouldn't even put a rope on Roy when he led the ponies to the lake.

Jeff-Kay Canipe is a dreamer like my parents. His goal in life is to own Bobby's Place, a store on the water on the other side of the lake. All you can buy at Bobby's Place is cold beer and gasoline, and when you pull up to the dock, one of Bobby's girls comes out to tie up your boat and take your order. All of Bobby's girls have big blond hair and dark tans and wear cutoff jeans and bikini tops and gold necklaces. Sometimes the bay is filled with assholes in Ski-Nautiques trying to hit on Bobby's girls. If the assholes aren't buying anything, Bobby comes out on the dock and shakes his fist and runs them off, and when they tear out of the bay the noses of their boats jump straight up out of the water and the engines roar like bears. There's going to be a bad boat wreck there someday. Jeff-Kay Canipe says that with any luck at all he'll be able to save enough money to make a down payment on Bobby's Place by the time he's forty. He's twenty-four now. He's already asked my parents to help him run it, although both of them will be close to eighty years old. Of course, they signed up. My mother says she'll wear a bikini. Jeff-Kay Canipe doesn't stop to think that Bobby's Place might be out of business then, or not for sale, that it might burn down, or that the dam could wash away during a flash flood and that Bobby's Place when he's forty might be sitting on the edge of a giant pasture. Jeff-Kay Canipe probably doesn't weigh 110 pounds, although the muscles in his arms and legs are knobby and he can run all day. His hair is thin already and combed back on top. He crinkles his eyes up when he thinks about what you've just said, and hugs my mother every time he comes to visit. He helps her wash dishes, and spins the plates on his finger. My mother says that Jeff-Kay Canipe and I could be twins, even though I'm six feet five and my hair is as thick as it ever was. I think, *Just enough to have knocked him down.* Sometimes Jeff-Kay Canipe sits at night with my parents in the lawn chairs around the pond and they talk about ways to improve the business once Bobby's Place becomes Canipe's General Store. Soft drinks, ice, suntan lotion, key chains that float, bottled air for scuba divers. They'll have to add on to the building. Build an additional dock. Hire more girls. Jeff-Kay Canipe dreams about the day in the future that Bobby's girls will become his. In 1973 he was a tiny boy with a stiff blond crew cut, and I watched him run out his front door and down through the yard faster and faster without a thought in his head. Now he dreams about standing on the edge of the dock at Canipe's General Store, while the Ski-Nautiques circle in the bay waiting their turn to buy something from him, and all around him are beautiful girls with soft brown skin that smells like coconut milk. Jeff-Kay Canipe's dream is *my* dream, in a way, because I watched out for him in 1973, but it's not a dream I can change, or make come true, and I don't want the responsibility of owning something I can't work on and fix. My parents point into the dark at the place on the other side of the trout pond where they say they're going to build a giant water slide.

The head gasket on my parents' generator is bad to blow, and I keep a spare one, and the tools I need to change it, in a box behind the seat of my truck. It's like being on call. My father's not much of a mechanic. The last time the gasket blew was late on a Saturday afternoon, and while I worked on the generator, my father rowed in the pond with the long crew oar that he uses to aerate the pond by hand. I don't have any idea where he found a crew oar in this part of the country, or even if you can aerate a pond by hand. I've always been able to get up there and fix the generator in time, and we haven't had to find out. That generator runs twenty-four hours a day, seven days a week, all year long. Someday it will give out for good and I won't be able to do a thing about it. My father has an oarlock mounted on a pole on the bank, and he marches four steps forward, pushing the oar through the water, then steps around it and marches four steps back. It was almost dark and my mother held a gas lantern over my shoulder while I worked. I think, *Five Thousand Trout*. I know the quiet when the generator's broken makes the trout nervous. Sometimes I think they're waiting for me to mess up. I can feel them all on my side of the pond, listening. Jeff-Kay Canipe was in the pasture playing with Dale. "Oh, Mama," my father said, "I feel like Ben-Hur."

"Ben-Hur," my mother said in her deepest voice, "I bring you both good news and bad news."

"Let me have the good news first."

"The good news is that every man will get an extra ration of bread and grog today during lunch."

"Oh, that's great news," my father said. "Thank the captain for me."

"Do you mean Lord Randall my son?"

"Yep," my father said. "He's the one."

"He says 'Thank you, Lord Randall,'" my mother said.

I think, *These people are my parents.*

"What's the bad news?" my father said.

"The bad news is that after lunch the captain wants to go water skiing."

"Oh, no," my father said. "Oh, no." He slapped the water twice with the oar. "Lord Randall is a sick man."

"I fear he is poisoned," my mother said.

I said, "That's not funny."

My mother giggled. "Ramming speed, Bud," she called out. "We pissed off Lord Randall."

"Tell him I'm weary with rowing and fain would lie down," my father said.

My mother held the lantern closer to the generator and looked down and sniffed. There was thick oil blown out all over the engine block. "Oh, dear," she said.

I said, "I can fix it this time. But next time, I don't know."

She leaned over and peered into the two open cylinders. I put the new gasket on the block and lined it up. My mother said, "Lake, I don't see how anyone ever learns how to be a doctor. I just don't."

Out in the pasture Roy whinnied once. Jeff-Kay Canipe wrapped his arms around Dale's neck and slid up onto her back. He pressed his knees against her sides and held on to her mane with both hands. She began to trot around the pasture, and Jeff-Kay Canipe bounced up and down on her back. Roy trotted alongside Dale, pressed up against Jeff-Kay Canipe's leg. Dale's head dropped a little each time she stepped with her sore front leg. "Yee-hah," my father yelled. "Ride 'em, Jeff-Kay."

My mother said, "Did you know that Jeff-Kay can spin a plate on his finger?"

I said, "Mama, tell Jeff-Kay Canipe to get off Dale."

My mother said, "He says it's all in the balance. That everything has a place where it balances, and he can feel where it is when he picks it up." She moved her arm up and down, testing the weight of the lantern. "Don't you think that's a lovely talent to have?"

I said, "Mama, Jeff-Kay Canipe's too big to be riding Dale like that."

"Oh, he's not," she said. "He's tiny. Dale likes it when he rides her."

I said, "He's going to break her down."

"You always think the worst," my mother said.

I think, *Somebody needs to around this place.*

My mother held up her hand. "Shh," she said.

I didn't hear anything except the hoofbeats of Dale and Roy, moving in a circle around the pasture, and the sound of my father rowing in the pond.

"Bud," my mother said. "Hold still."

My father pulled his oar up out of the water. "What is it?" he said.

"Listen," my mother said.

Off in the distance then I heard voices, at first what seemed like hundreds of them, singing light and high.

The sweat turned icy on my back.

"What?" my father said.

"The Girl Scouts," my mother said.

I stood up and turned around and looked down my parents' driveway. In the road, 150 yards away, a troop of Girl Scouts was marching by in the dark. I could just barely make out their white shirts. I heard,

> *Hang down your head Tom Dooley*
> *Hang down your head and cry*
> *Hang down your head Tom Dooley*
> *Poor boy you're bound to die.*

My mother held the lantern over her head and waved it back and forth, as if she were signaling for help. Out in the road a single flashlight blinked on and pointed down the driveway. My mother waved. I heard,

> *I met her on the mountain*
> *And there I took her life*
> *I met her on the mountain*
> *And stabbed her with my knife*

Out in the road the flashlight blinked out. The sound of the voices got smaller and smaller, going away. "Oh, Lake," my mother said. "Did you hear that? They sing like angels." Down the road the Girl Scouts started another verse, but I couldn't make out the words. Behind me I heard Jeff-Kay Canipe say "Whoa," and the hoofbeats in the pasture dwindled down and stopped. I turned back around and looked at the generator. I don't know why, but for a second when I looked down into the blackness of the cylinders I felt like I was going to fall in and keep falling. "Oh, I'm so happy that thing wasn't running," my mother said. My father had his long oar poised above the pond, waiting, and when I looked up he waved like we didn't have a thing in the world to worry about. Not a thing. My mother started to hum. In the pasture Jeff-Kay Canipe hugged Dale and bent down to look at her leg. Lightning bugs blinked all around us, and the water in the pond was still, still, still.

ALICEVILLE

WE SAW the geese from the road at dusk, a flock
of maybe forty or fifty. They dropped suddenly out of
the sky, miles from the nearest flyway, and landed in a
bottom on one of our farms, just outside Aliceville,
North Carolina. This was in December, on one of those
still evenings in the new part of winter when you cannot
decide whether it is a good thing to inhale deeply, the
air is so clear and sharp.

Uncle Zeno and I were headed home — I don't
remember now where we had been — and the geese
came down on us like a revelation: a single gray and
black goose shot from out of nowhere directly into the
path of our truck, flying faster than you would imagine
anything that big could fly. It was so low to the ground
that we heard the whistle of its wings over the sound of
the engine. And before we were even through jumping
in our seats, the air around us exploded with honking
geese, so close and flying so fast that they seemed in
danger of crashing into the truck. Their rising shouts

and the rushing sound of their wings, coming on us so suddenly, were as loud and frightening as unexpected gunshots, and as strange to our ears as ancient tongues. Uncle Zeno slammed on the brakes so hard that the truck fishtailed in the gravel and left us crosswise in the road, facing the bottom.

The geese flew across the field and turned in a climbing curve against the wooded ridge on the other side of the creek, back the way they had come, toward Uncle Zeno and me. They spread out their great wings, beating straight downward in short strokes, catching themselves in the air, and settled into the short corn stubble, probably a half mile from the road. And they disappeared then, in the middle of the field as we watched, through the distance and the dim winter light, as completely as if they had been ghosts. Uncle Zeno turned off the headlights, and then the engine, and we leaned forward and stared out into the growing darkness, until the ridge was black against the sky. Canadian geese just did not on an ordinary day fly over the small place in which we lived our lives. We did not speak at first, and listened to our blood, and the winter silence around us, and wondered at the thing we had seen.

We decided on the way home, the sounds of flight still wild in our ears, that the geese bedded down in the bottom would be our secret, one that we would not share with Uncle Coran and Uncle Al, who were Uncle Zeno's brothers. My uncles were close, but they were competitive in the way that brothers often are — they could not fish or hunt without keeping score — and

Uncle Zeno said that we could get a good one over on Uncle Coran and Uncle Al, who were twins, if we walked in at breakfast the next morning carrying a brace of Canadian geese. He hoped that we could sneak up on the flock just before dawn, while they were still bedded and cold, and thought that he could drop two, maybe three if he could reload fast enough, before they managed to get into the air and climb away from the bottom. He was as excited on the way home as I had ever seen him.

My mother was also to be excluded from our plans, because Uncle Zeno said that if she even looked at Uncle Coran and Uncle Al, they would know something was up, and would gang up on her until she told them our secret. My mother was fourteen years younger than Uncle Al and Uncle Coran, and twenty-one years younger than Uncle Zeno. They called her Sissy, and knew — even after she was a grandmother, and they were men of ancient and remarkable age — exactly what to say to make her mad enough to fight. It was impossible for her to lie to them about anything. We lived with Uncle Zeno on Depot Street, and Uncle Coran and Uncle Al lived on either side of us, in houses of their own. The five of us together ate as a family three times a day, at the long table in Uncle Zeno's dining room, meals that my mother cooked.

I managed to keep quiet about the geese during supper, although Uncle Coran and Uncle Al more than once commented on the possum-like nature of my grin. Uncle Zeno twice nudged me under the table with his foot, and narrowed his eyes in warning. The whole family knew something was up, and that Uncle Zeno was behind it. I enjoyed every minute of letting them know that I knew what it was. It was a position I was not often in. My mother slipped into my room that night after I went to bed, bearing in her apron a rare stick of peppermint. She broke it in two and presented me with half, which I accepted. We sucked on our candy in silence, staring at each other, until she asked, misjudging my allegiances, just what exactly Uncle Zeno and I were up to. I told her that we were going to see a man about a dog, which is what Uncle Zeno would have said in reply to such a transparent attempt at bribery. My mother smiled — she always considered it a good sign to see parts of her brothers, particularly parts of Uncle Zeno, coming out in me — and told me to make sure that the dog would bark at a stranger, which was one of the many appropriate responses. After she kissed me and left the room, I heard Uncle Zeno in the kitchen loudly proclaiming that he didn't know what in the world they were talking about, that we weren't up to anything at all.

That night on their way back to their houses, Uncle Coran and Uncle Al stopped outside my window, pressed their faces against the glass, and growled like bears. I treated their performance with the disdain it deserved. I could not know then what the next day would bring, what Uncle Zeno and I would discover on our hunt. Most of the things that make you see the world and yourself in it differently, you do not imagine beforehand, and I suppose that is the best way. It enables us to live moment to moment in the things we hope to be true. I went to sleep that night possessor, along with my uncle, of what we thought to be a magnificent secret: in the morning a flock of Canadian geese would rise up before us into the air. They would be waiting, there in the frozen field, when we sneaked up on them in the new light.

In what seemed like only minutes, Uncle Zeno pulled my toe and held a finger to his lips. It was dark outside, for all I knew the deepest part of the night. I thought briefly about going back to sleep, into the dreams I had traveled through, and whose thresholds were still close by, but the thought of the geese exploding into the air, the secret adventure that I would share with Uncle Zeno, brought me fully awake. I kicked back the covers and gathered up my clothes and shoes and ran into the kitchen to dress beside the fire. Uncle Zeno was already wearing his hunting coat, and the legs of his overalls were stuffed down into the tall, black rubber boots he wore when he fed the stock. He was grinning. "Get a move on, Doc," he whispered, blowing on a cup of coffee. "Tonight me and you'll be eating a big old goose for dinner. You think we should let anybody else have any?" His shotgun was broken open and lying on the table. Neither his stock boots nor the gun, by my mother's decree, were supposed to be in the kitchen. I shook my head no. Let the rest of the world find their own geese.

When I was dressed, still shivering from my dash between sleep and the fire, Uncle Zeno and I started down the hall toward the darkness outside, and the things that waited for us in it, most of which we did not know. As we tiptoed past my mother's open door, she coughed, which stopped Uncle Zeno in his tracks. He shifted his gun to the other hand and dragged me by the collar back into the kitchen. From out of the straw basket that sat on the second shelf of the cupboard, he removed a piece of corn bread left over from supper the night before. "Here, Doc," he said, "you better eat this." He also poured me a glass of buttermilk. I gulped it all down. When we passed my mother's room a second time, we didn't hear a thing.

Once we made it out of the house, Uncle Zeno and I left in a hurry, pausing only long enough to scrape the ice off the windshield. If Uncle Al and Uncle Coran heard the sound of the truck starting in the yard, they did not dash barefoot out of their houses to see where we were going. And if our flight woke any of the hounds and pointers and assorted feists that divided their time and allegiances between our three houses, they did not crawl from out of their beds beneath the porches to investigate. We escaped cleanly, down the single block of Depot Street to the state highway.

Aliceville was still asleep as far as I could tell, the houses dark, and before Uncle Zeno even finished shifting into high gear we were out of town completely and into the open country. There is a surveyor's iron stake driven into the ground underneath the depot that marks the exact center of Aliceville — I suppose that small boys still play games whose rules involve crawling through the spiderwebs and imagined snakes beneath the building to touch the stake, there at the center of things — and from that point the imaginary line marking the city limits is only a half mile away in any direction. Aliceville is a small but perfect circle on a map, and it sits in the middle of the fields that surround it like a small idea in danger of being forgotten. We lived our lives inside that circle, and made it a town by saying that it was.

The stars were still bright and close above us, but strange somehow, stopped at some private point in their spinning that I had never seen. The state highway was white in the beams of our headlights, and black beyond, and the expansion strips in the concrete bumped under our tires in the countable rhythm of distance passing. There was no sign yet of the coming day, although in the east, down close to the tops of the trees beyond the fields, there was a faint purple tint that disappeared if you stared at it very long and tried, in your wishing for light and warmth, to turn it into dawn. The fields beside the highway were white with a hard frost.

Two miles outside town, Uncle Zeno turned off the state highway onto the dirt road that ran past the bottom where the geese waited for us in the dark. He cut the headlights and slowed the truck to a stealthy crawl, the engine barely above idle. We crept along the road in the starlight until he stopped the truck and turned off the engine a mile or more away from the bottom, at the place where the creek that ran on the other side of it

forded the road. "Don't slam the door, Doc," Uncle
Zeno whispered. "From here on out, if we poot, they'll
hear it. If we make a sound, we'll never see them."

Uncle Zeno loaded his double barrel with two shells
out of the pocket of his hunting coat, and gingerly
clicked it shut. We were going to sneak up on the flock
by walking in the creek, which had high banks and was
hidden from view on both sides by thick underbrush.
When we got close enough, we would run up out of the
brush like Indians, and into the middle of the sleeping
geese. They would explode into the frozen air around us
for Uncle Zeno to shoot. I did not have any rubber
boots, so I climbed onto Uncle Zeno's back — my uncles
were tall, strong men who ran their last footrace down
Depot Street on Uncle Zeno's sixtieth birthday — and I
looped my arms around his neck and my legs around his
waist. He shrugged once to get me higher on his back,
and stepped over the thick mush ice that grew up out of
the bank, and into the cold creek.

Uncle Zeno carried his gun in his right hand, and I
felt its stock against my hip. We moved slowly downstream, and in a few steps the brush and trees that grew
on the sides of the creek closed above our heads and hid
us from whatever might have been watching. Uncle
Zeno slid each foot in and out of the creek so quietly
that I could not distinguish his steps from the noise
made by the water.

We ducked beneath low-hanging vines and limbs and
the trunks of trees that had fallen across the creek. I

looked up through the thick branches and vines that were tangled above our heads, and could only occasionally see a star. They were dimmer, though it was still night, than when we had left home. I rested my chin on Uncle Zeno's shoulder and closed my eyes and listened to the sound of the creek moving by us in the dark. I might've even dozed off. When I opened my eyes I could sense the bottom on my left, its openness beneath the sky, but I could not see it yet through the laurel and briars. We were still a long way from the geese. Uncle Zeno tilted his head back until the stubble of his beard brushed my cheek, and he said "Shh" so softly that I almost couldn't hear it.

To this day, I do not know what sound we made that caused the geese to fly — how they knew we were there. We never saw them. We were still four or five hundred yards away when they took off, but I knew when it happened it was because of something we had done. We had been silly to think we could get close. When they rose from the bottom their wings pushing against the air sounded like a hard rain, one that might wake you up in the middle of the night. Their shouted cries were as exotic and urgent as they had been the night before, and I heard inside those cries frozen places we would never see. Uncle Zeno and I didn't move when they went up — we were so far away that it didn't startle us, but seemed inevitable somehow — and we stood still in the creek, with our heads cocked upward, listening. We could hear them a long time after they took off, spiraling upward in the sky, calling out, until they were high above us, almost out of earshot, and leaving our part of the world for good.

We listened to those last fading calls until even the possibility of hearing them again was gone, until not even our wishing could keep the familiar sounds we tried not to hear from returning into our lives. The creek moved around us as if we weren't there, along the edge of the bottom toward the river. A truck bound for New Carpenter on the state highway downshifted in the distance. A dog barked. I hid my face against Uncle Zeno's neck, suddenly ashamed of what we had wanted to do, of the dark thing we had held in our hearts. At that moment I would have said a prayer to bring the geese back, to hide them again in the field, had I thought it would work. But I knew there was nothing I could do, no desperate bargain I could make, that it was over, just over. The simple presence of the geese had made our world seem less small, and we were smaller than we had been, once they were gone.

When Uncle Zeno finally moved, I was surprised to see that it was daylight. The trunks of the trees around us had changed from black to gray, as if the day had been waiting only for the geese to climb back into the sky. I could make out the faint red of the sand on the bottom of the creek, the dark green of the laurel on its banks. It was like waking up. Uncle Zeno let out a long breath and turned toward the bottom and waded out of the creek. I slid down onto the ground. "Well, Doc," he

said, "I guess me and you might as well go on home."
Through the undergrowth I saw the gray sky curving
down toward the field. Somewhere a crow called out a
warning. There was nothing remarkable about any of it,
not that I could tell, not anymore.

STORY OF PICTURES

WHEN I WAS A BOY, my room faced a railroad track and a streetlight. The long freight from Hamlet came through town just after midnight, and I tried to stay awake so I could listen to it pound by in the dark, bound for the switching yard at Gunter, and Erwin, Tennessee, on the other side of the mountains, and Elkhorn City, Kentucky, far away at the end of the line. More often than not I went to sleep thinking about that train, and when I slept, I rode the Seaboard Air Line from Aliceville, North Carolina, to the places of my dreams.

My bed was in the middle of the floor, between the window facing the track and the window the streetlight painted on my wall, and when the westbound pushed through, the dark shapes of steam engines and boxcars flashed by, and I could reach out and touch them with my hand. One night the shadow of a man slid by, twisting in a square of light, and I pulled the covers over my head.

On the nights I couldn't stay awake, I heard the train in my sleep, and felt our house shake as it passed. Some mornings I woke strange with the feeling that I had slept on a rocking car, and that I had come a long way under the stars to get back home. I remember how my mother leaned over my bed in the morning and how she smiled when I opened my eyes, how the house was strange and quiet after the noise of my journey, and how the air was thick with the smell of biscuits and coffee and ham; I can remember the low voices of my uncles as they talked around the kitchen table about the coming day, and how my mother touched my forehead and said in a low voice I knew she saved for me: "Where have you been, Jimmy Glass? Where did you go, dreamy boy?" While I ate breakfast she went through the house and straightened the pictures hanging on the walls.

Aliceville during the Depression measured time in arrivals and departures. The Hamlet to New Carpenter local stopped in the morning at 9:50, and again on its way home, and we got mail twice a day. The old steam engine had a cowcatcher like the brim of an engineer's hat, and it pulled four green cars with gold letters on their sides. You could ride the local to New Carpenter and back for fifty cents, or Hamlet and back for a dollar. Drummers rode it almost every day of the week, east and west, going and coming. They walked the streets weighted down on one side with black sample cases full of new deals. Down the street from the depot, hard by the track, was the skinny brick hotel where they stayed.

The salesman from Statesville Feeds carried a pocketful of rock candy, and every kid in town knew who he was and when he would be back.

The freight from Elkhorn City pulled in at noon and took on water, and its engines panted on the siding and chuffed black smoke. The eastbound sitting still was considerably longer than the town, and it stretched out of sight into the country. When its whistle blew men walked in from the fields for their dinner, and when it blew again they pushed their chairs back from the table. It dumped mountains of coal at the depot and a narrow-gauge company train hauled the coal a car at a time to the cotton mills across the river at Roberta and Allendale. The coal train pulled into town headfirst and then backed all the way home, and any self-respecting boy could outrun it for fifty or sixty yards at a time.

My father, Jim Glass, died of a heart attack a week before I was born, and my mother and I lived with her oldest brother, Zeno McBride, on Depot Street, between Uncle Al's and Uncle Coran's. Uncle Zeno inherited the McBride family homeplace when my grandparents died. Uncle Coran and Uncle Al were twins, and when the family businesses prospered during the First World War, they moved out of Uncle Zeno's and built houses identical to it on either side. In the evenings after supper, we all sat together on Uncle Zeno's front porch, except during the occasional family disagreement, when my uncles would sit alone, each on his own porch. None of them ever got married. Uncle Al grew cotton and tobacco, and Uncle Coran ran the cotton gin and the feed store.

Uncle Zeno operated the gristmill on Painter Creek, and Mother fretted and tried to look out after the whole bunch of us. Her name was Elizabeth, and my uncles called her Sissy, even when they were old men whose hands shook underneath the hats in their laps and she was an old woman who couldn't remember their names.

My uncles were tall, skinny, hawk-nosed men who seemed older than they were, until they became old, and then they seemed younger than everyone else their age. They spoke softly around my mother, who would cry without provocation but tried not to, and they were good to me. They made sure that I didn't have to work hard, or at least no harder than I wanted to work, and on my ninth birthday Uncle Coran and Uncle Al drove all the way to Charlotte and brought back a pinto pony named Skip. Uncle Zeno produced a saddle with pictures of Indian chiefs tooled into the leather, and a set of real saddlebags that he ordered from Texas. I think the fact that the saddlebags came from Texas pleased Uncle Zeno almost as much as it did me. During the long, slow summers Skip and I had the run of the place, and we ranged far and wide.

Most mornings I saddled Skip and rode west along the tracks to meet the eastbound. Sometimes I tied a red bandana around my face and whooped and hollered and raced Skip alongside the train like I was Jesse James. Other times I just sat by the tracks with my forearm across the saddle horn and watched it go by. Skip wasn't afraid of trains, and he stood with his front feet on the gravel of the roadbed and paid no attention while the long freight roared by almost close enough to touch.

When the eastbound passed, I stared straight ahead and waited for empty cars. If a car was open, a square of light skimmed along the ground in the train's shadow, and I could see it coming through the corner of my eye. When the car passed, Skip and I were bathed for an instant in the moving light; in front of us the cotton fields and woods and sky on the other side of the track were framed like giant pictures. The pictures were tall and wide, and they flashed and were gone in the same heartbeat, and there was always more to look at than I had time to see. I could change the picture by turning my head a little before the next open car banged by, and the everyday world seemed magic somehow when I looked at it that way. I halfway believed that one day I would glimpse Cherokee braves running naked along the far edge of the field, their long black hair flying out behind them, or redcoats marching to Kings Mountain behind Colonel Ferguson in a powdered wig, or Confederate cavalry charging on ragged mounts; I halfway expected that one day, through the flashing doors, I would see my mother as a little girl on her way to school, or my father hoeing cotton in the sun, and if someone asked me at dinner why I was so quiet, that was why.

Most afternoons I rode Skip out to Uncle Zeno's mill. My great-grandfather Mauney McBride built the mill after he came home from the Civil War, just below where Painter Creek rushes down off Lynn's Mountain and slows and widens on its way to the river. The tall, thin dam was made out of rock, and it was hidden in the woods across the road. A wide lip of boards ran across the top of the dam, and the runoff fell out away from its face, and there was room to stand between the dam and the falling water. A race connected the pond to the millhouse, and a short wooden bridge crossed the race. Uncle Zeno whitewashed the millhouse every spring after planting, and one year he hired a man from Shelby to paint the word "McBride" across the side of the building in tall black letters. The water wheel was fifteen feet tall and made of iron, and during the summer I walked in the bottom of it while it turned, and the cold water fell all around me, and inside the millhouse the great gears grumbled like the belly of a giant beast.

When I was eighteen, I put on my only suit and boarded the local with four other boys and went off to the war. I told the Army that I knew about trains and they told me I was a fireman and sent me overseas. I shoveled coal on shrill-whistled foreign freights that hauled fresh troops and artillery and tanks east across Europe, and soldiers in various states of disrepair in the other direction. I wasn't as homesick as most soldiers because the trains I fired sounded like home, and because the coal I shoveled was black like the coal the little company train backed across the river to Roberta and Allendale, and because I somehow believed that all railroad tracks were connected.

It was easy to imagine in Belgium and France that around the next bend would be Uncle Al's house and then our house, and then Uncle Coran's, all three white and tin-roofed and stern, with windows facing the track, and that I could look inside each as I passed and see a train filled with lights crossing the wall; it was easy to picture the narrow red streets opening up one at a time like tunnels until I could see the cotton fields spreading out at their ends; it was easy to believe, even in Germany in 1945, that one morning I would wake up and hear my uncles talking in the kitchen, and my mother would lean over my bed and brush my hair back with a finger and whisper, "Where have you been, Jimmy Glass?" and that for the first time I could say where the train had taken me in the night.

When I came back home, I joined the Great Southeastern Railway as a fireman, and I married an Aliceville girl named Christine and I fired doomed and handsome black engines through the last days of steam; and then I was an engineer on ugly diesel monsters with power enough to light cities, pulling two hundred cars at a time as fast as the law would let me, and my daughters went to school in Columbia and Greensboro and Meridian and Charlotte and Norfolk and grew up; and then I was a district supervisor in charge of 712 miles of Southeastern track, and my daughters married fine boys whose names I still mix up, and I rode trains for sometimes thirty days at a stretch, and my wife and I bought and lived in houses I never learned to navigate in the dark, and it all happened just like that.

On May 14, 1983, in the small hours of the morning,

my heart stopped on board a long freight racing daylight in south Georgia, and they lifted me off at a crossing south of St. Marys. The train was rolling again before the ambulance driver slammed the door, and by the time it got to Jacksonville, it was only four minutes late. Through the rear window of the ambulance, I saw red lights shoot out and die in the black Georgia night. These are the things I dreamed about, and the things I dream about still:

Uncle Zeno's millpond was the best swimming hole in the country, and the most popular. It was as beautiful there as any promised land you could imagine. The branches of tall maple trees closed high above it, and thick, shiny laurel walled it in on the sides. A long rope with a stirrup on one end was tied to a limb overhanging the deepest part, and several generations of Aliceville mothers made their children swear they wouldn't swing on it. The water was green as a jewel, and it moved toward the dam so slow that it didn't seem to move at all, and it fell away clear as glass and shattered on the rocks below. The sun came through the trees only in spots, and the spots moved on the surface of the pond when the wind blew, and even during the hottest months the water was icy cold. Men showered in the runoff from the dam when they finished working in the fields on Saturdays, and they hooted and whooped in the cold water. They kept stiff brushes and bars of Octagon soap hidden in the cracks between the rocks, and they scrubbed with the brushes until their skins were red and

the water below the dam ran muddy. On Sunday afternoons the pond boiled and flashed with naked boys, and
the air was filled with their shouts.

During the week, while the other boys carried fertil-
izer or hoed cotton, I swam in the pond alone. Sometimes I dove down and felt the cold rock of the dam with
my hands, and pushed against it, and imagined the high,
open space not more than a foot away and the water
falling through it and breaking on the rocks and forming
again into Painter Creek and moving off toward the
river like nothing had happened. Sometimes I swam
along the bottom like a catfish, moving my wide head
back and forth. The bottom was muddy and covered
with slick leaves. Other days I swung on the rope and
watched my reflection fly on the water below, and I tried
to dive from the rope so that I could see a picture of
myself flying up through the green water. Sometimes I
floated on my back and stared up, and the trees closed
over my head like the roof of a cathedral, and some days
it all made me feel the way I was supposed to feel in
church.

One afternoon when I was ten or eleven, a woman I
had never seen before walked out of the woods. I heard
her coming in time and slithered into the laurel on the
far side of the pond. She wore khaki work pants and
heavy boots and a man's gray shirt, and the shirt and
pants were too big. She carried a tall, black tripod with
a heavy camera mounted on top. Her hair was stuffed
up under a brown felt hat like the one Uncle Zeno wore,
and the band of the hat was ringed with sweat. Her shirt

was circled under the arms. It was the hottest part of a Depression summer. She stepped close to the water and spread the legs of the tripod and stuck them into the sand. She tugged at the front of the camera and it extended like an accordion. The lens stared across the pond like an alert, blue eye, and I covered myself with my hand.

She twisted a dial on the front of the camera, and she raised her arm and moved her hand back and forth, and studied it in the light. She shook her head and said something to herself, but I couldn't hear what it was. She looked slowly around the pond, and back up the path, and then she took off her hat and hung it on the extended lens, and something about the way she did it made my heart jump. She drew three hairpins out of her hair, and stuck them in the band of her hat. She spread her fingers wide and pulled them through her hair. It was long and yellow, and it fell down around her shoulders. I stared at her from my hiding place, part of me afraid that she wasn't real and the rest of me afraid that she was. I had believed that only women in the Bible could have been beautiful the way she was beautiful; I don't think I would have been more surprised if Ruth or Mary or Eve had walked out of the laurel and filled an earthen jug with water.

Several years before, a solar eclipse darkened the sky over Aliceville, and my third-grade teacher, Mrs. Weaver, pulled the blinds and told a story about a little girl who had been mesmerized by an eclipse. The little girl only wanted to peek at it, but once she saw it she couldn't look away. She stared at it until it blinded her, and all she saw for the rest of her life was a burning black sun. As the morning shadows slid from the blackboard and died on the floor, and Mrs. Weaver's classroom became dark, the green light of a dream filtered in around the blinds, and I felt the awful pull of the eclipse. I wanted to run to the back of the room and jerk the blinds off the windows and stare up into the dark sun until it was all I could see. I tell this now because that's how I felt at the pond when I watched the photographer swim. She might as well have been the sun. I couldn't have looked away to save my sight.

She walked to the edge of the water and stopped there. The shadows of her ribs swept up from her stomach and curved beneath her breasts. Her skin was smooth and white, and I had never seen anything so lovely. Her reflection stretched out beneath her, and when she stuck her toe into the pond, a white foot seemed to rise up out of the water and meet her foot in the air. She walked into the water and held out her arms, and the reflection reached up. The water rose above her waist, and she slid forward into the waiting arms, and disappeared beneath the surface of the pond. She came up beneath the rope and rolled onto her back, and her arms rose up from her sides one at a time and moved in slow arcs like the hands of a clock. One arm drew half a circle in the air and disappeared into the water behind her head, and the other arm rose and followed. She swam to the dam, and held on to the top of it with her hands and peered over the side. I wished then that I was in the pond with her, watching the water fall through the air.

She drew her feet up underneath her, and pushed off against the side of the dam, and slid through the pond and stopped in front of me. To this day, I don't know if she saw me, or what she was thinking, but she stared straight into the laurel and smiled. Her eyes were as green as the water. The tops of her breasts were jeweled with drops of water. Her arms moved out from her sides, and in toward her breasts, and back out again. She closed her eyes and shook her head from side to side, and her long hair flew out in a circle, and it wrapped around her face and unwrapped, and wrapped again. Bright drops of water flew out in lines from her hair and crossed in the air and fell and circled the surface of the pond. The circles grew and crossed, and more drops fell, and for an instant the water shivered and glowed and nothing at all seemed very real.

Then she swam across the pond, climbed out of the water, re-pinned her hair, and dressed. She put on her hat, picked up her camera, and disappeared into the woods. I dove back into the pond. The water was so cold that it made my teeth chatter, but I stayed in it a long time. I thought about the water she swam in going over the side of the dam, and down Painter Creek into the river, and down the river into the ocean; I thought about a white beach stretching away from where the river disappeared into the sea, and I imagined the calls of seabirds flying over the water, and I wondered if I would ever see her again, or if I had seen her at all. Back at the mill, Uncle Zeno grinned and asked me if I had seen a woman swimming over there, and I said no, I hadn't seen any woman swimming, and he studied my face for a second and didn't say anything else about it. That evening at supper, he told Mother that a lady photographer from the WPA stopped and took a picture of the mill. Six months later, he got an envelope in the mail from Washington, D.C., but the bottom was ripped out of it and there was nothing inside.

After that, I noticed how the streets of Aliceville ran out into the cotton fields and stopped. I thought about how tiny the town must look to a bird, or somebody in an airplane. It seemed to me then that the place I was born was as plain and fragile as a piece of notebook paper on a red playground, and that it would have blown away across the fields long ago if it hadn't been strapped to the ground by a railroad track.

When I closed my eyes that night, all I saw was the woman I had seen at the pond. I thought about her green eyes, and her long hair, and how her long, white hands moved through the water toward her breasts again and again. I couldn't sleep, and when the westbound came through at midnight, I got out of bed and pressed against the window painted on my wall, and I felt the moving shadows and shapes and lights. I closed my eyes, and she beckoned to me from the water, and I thought that maybe she called my name. The train roared and banged on through the night, on the way to somewhere else, and I wanted it to go faster and faster.

MY FATHER'S HEART

My MOTHER AND I lived on Depot Street with her oldest brother, Zeno McBride, and Uncle Al and Uncle Coran, who were twins, lived on either side of us in houses that were identical to ours. In the evenings after supper, the five of us sat together on Uncle Zeno's front porch until the stars grew bright in the sky. My mother and uncles rarely spoke of my father during the day, but he appeared almost nightly in their voices and wandered through the stories they told. Over the years I sat at my mother's feet and listened as he became as perfect as a dream. Whenever my mother talked about my father, she stared straight ahead at pictures only she could see, things she remembered, and things she imagined, and described what she saw until I could see it too, as clearly as if I had been there. In her stories the events of June 1924 took on the importance of an Easter offered to the two of us, and not to the rest of the world.

Even when I was twice the age of my father when he died, and my daughters, her grandchildren, were older than she was when she was widowed, my mother looked at me and saw my father's face. And even as she disappeared into the white center of a hospital bed, arguing with men my uncles and I could not see and had never met, over debts she did not owe, I could not look into her eyes without seeing the still reflection of my father's ghost. She came to believe early, and with all conviction, that she would have only one story to tell, that only one story was possible in a life. I was the one she picked, even as her brothers buried her husband, to provide her story with an ending. At her funeral, her minister said that the faithfulness and clarity of her vision was her greatest gift, but I do not think it was a gift. My mother's most terminal illness was the failure of her imagination. She never remarried, and grew old taking care of her bachelor brothers in the tall rooms of the three stern houses.

My father, Jim Ray Glass, Sr., died one week before I was born. He went out to hoe cotton the morning of June 8, 1924, and when he didn't come home for dinner, Uncle Al went out and found him flat on his back in the field, staring up in stiff, glazed wonder at the sky. Uncle Al squatted in the row and with his hat brushed the red ants off my father's face until Uncle Coran found the two of them an hour later. Uncle Coran ran home for Uncle Zeno and the wagon, and the three of them carried my father out of the field and brought him back to town and laid his body on Uncle Al's kitchen table.

The women of Aliceville wiped their hands on their aprons when they heard, and rushed to Uncle Zeno's house, where they put my mother to bed and kept her there until after I was born. That first afternoon they drew the blinds of the room where my mother lay, and sent to Uncle Zeno's ice house for a big block of ice. They wiped her face with cold cloths, and told her how lucky she was that Jim Glass had given her a child. They placed their hands on my mother's stomach and nodded when I kicked.

Their husbands came in early from the fields and sat on Uncle Al's front porch in their overalls, quietly smoking, their hats pulled down low, and told and retold Uncle Al's story. My father had squeezed his work shirt and overalls into a ball over his heart, as if the weight of the cloth was crushing him. In the kitchen my three uncles bathed my father and wrapped him in an ironed white sheet. The doctor came that night and signed the death certificate and checked in on my mother. Her nurses sat in straight chairs against the walls, their eyes hidden in the deep shadows made by the kerosene light. I was born Jim Ray Glass, Jr., one week later, on June 15, 1924.

In the months following my father's death, the women of Aliceville did their best to keep my mother company. They made a fuss over me and listened with sympathy to her grieving, until her story gradually began to diverge from what they remembered as the truth. Then they one by one pronounced her queer for not getting on with her life, and whispered among themselves about how it had been a mistake to keep Sissy Glass from seeing Jim Glass buried. My uncles, although well-respected in the community, were also considered a little out of the ordinary by Aliceville standards, and therefore vaguely suspect, partly because they never married, and partly because of their houses, which were distinguishable from the outside only by their position on the street. As a boy I got into more than one playground fight defending my uncles' singular taste in architecture, and my mother's strange and permanent grief.

By the time I started to school, my mother had only my uncles and me to listen to her story, but eventually my uncles, who even as old men continued to watch over her with the awkward love of proud boys for a baby sister, began to move through her words as easily as they did through the air that carried them. And then, as the meaning of her story sharpened in her mind into something she had to repeat to believe, my mother turned solely to me. And I listened. From the time that I was a small boy, until she died, when I was forty-six — even though for most of that time I realized that what my mother remembered about my father was hopelessly entangled with what she imagined — her stories about him never failed to fill me with great sadness at her loss. In that way, at least, I can truthfully say that I was a good son. My mother was an unflinching Christian, and believed that if she had been chosen to carry a burden, it had to be for a good reason. She shifted under it and rearranged it and struggled with it until the day she died. When I was a child, I never knew when my mother would cry, only that I somehow had helped cause it, and

I entered the rooms where she sat with an apology formed on my lips like a prayer. Every small kindness I did my mother, she repaid by telling me I had my father's heart.

I have often wondered since what inadvertently unkind words I have spoken to my daughters, and if those words have shaped frightening dreams. My mother, who died in 1970, never knew about the nights I lay in my bed in Uncle Zeno's house with my hand on my chest, while the freight from Hamlet clanged by and lights swirled around the room, sure beyond doubt that she would find me dead when she came to wake me in the morning; she never knew that I was as sure my heart would stop with each passing beat as I was sure that each boxcar as it passed would be the last of the train, until finally one was; and she never knew, those countless times she saw my father living in me, and imagined some great deed that I would someday do, the grand ending I would make for her story, and reached out and touched my face and smiled, how ultimately right her declaration would be. My heart is diseased beyond repair or hope; my hands shake in anticipation. More than one doctor has told me that I am lucky to be alive. If I walk in the morning to the mailbox I have to lean against it and rest before I can walk back. Each breath I draw requires intricate negotiations. The medicine I take to make my blood thin has made me impotent, and some nights the warm smell of my wife, Christine, sleeping fills me with a sorrow like a black tunnel, through which I think I'll never pass.

This morning Christine glanced at me once and rushed away to the grocery store, filled, I'm sure, with her own constant and private dread. When I die, I do not want her to be the one to find me. I do not want to figure sadly in the stories she has to tell. The half hour she was gone I sat alone in the sun on our porch, and all around me the world was filled with beating hearts: a vain young cardinal fought himself to exhaustion in the mirror of my truck; a school bus climbed the hill past our house spilling the ghostly laughter and shouts of children; our mailman as he drove away from our box threw up his hand in solitary greeting and camaraderie. I was delighted to wave back. I tell myself that the beauty of the life around me — these little things — is what makes me lucky to be alive, that it allows me to stack my days the way a child stacks blocks — to impossible, swaying heights that make the breath catch.

My grandchildren are all very small, and when their mothers bring them to visit, they totter across the yard toward me, the earth new and unsteady beneath their feet, their arms held out to life. But always, even in my happiest moments, with an internal ear I listen to my father's heart beat inside my chest. My heart is a paper bag full of blood, pumping, pumping. My blood seeps through the thinning walls, around the weakening seams, and one day it will break, the bottom will fall out, and that will be that. The stacked blocks of my days will topple toward some distant, final floor, and I will see in that bright instant as they fall what it was my young father saw — the true thing he gazed at that day in 1924 when he lay flat on his back and stared up at the sky; the vision that put the look of wonder on his face that Uncle Al looked down on while he brushed away, with the felt brim of his hat, the red ants that came for my father. Uncle Al told me once, before he died in 1974, that he had seen a story trapped in my father's eyes.

Jim Glass came to Aliceville in December 1918, when he was seventeen years old. Half of the town was down with influenza, and fourteen people out of a population of a little less than two hundred, including both of my maternal grandparents, did not live to see the spring. Uncle Zeno, who suddenly found himself the head of the family businesses, and shorthanded, hired my father to do odd jobs around the cotton gin and feed store and gristmill until the regular help got back on their feet. He lived that first winter in the storeroom of the cotton gin, which despite its lack of creature comforts at least had a stove and a steady supply of coal. All three of my uncles liked my father, who they said worked hard despite a dreamy streak — sometimes he looked right at them while they talked but didn't hear a word they said — and they kept him on in the spring to help with the planting, and then in the summer to help with the hoeing, and then in the fall to help with the harvest and the ginning, and then finally bought a tenant house on the outskirts of town and rented it to him for two dollars a month.

At first my father's presence in Aliceville caused no small amount of concern among the good people of the town. If you take a sharp stick and draw a circle around country people and tell them that inside the circle is town, they instantly become disdainful and suspicious of their neighbors who still live outside it. They thought it was bad enough that young Jim Glass came from Lynn's Mountain — an uncivilized place, it was said, where even the preachers didn't wear shoes and everybody was related to everybody else — but what really caused their consternation was the fact that his father was the bootlegger Amos Glass, who was well-known for his letters to the editor of the *Charlotte Observer* advocating a second secession, and for turning, by secret process, the fruit of the wild cherry trees on the sides of Lynn's Mountain into his famous Cherry Bounce. For a time after Reconstruction, Amos Glass's Cherry Bounce sold for as much as twenty-five dollars a gallon and was served in the back rooms of the finest hotels in Asheville and Charlotte and Columbia.

Amos Glass was a vain, ambitious man — and a truly gifted distiller — and when late in the last century the demand for his Cherry Bounce and Clear Glass Special Moon far exceeded his ability to produce it, he spent his fortune on a modern, brick distillery high up on the side of Lynn's Mountain. The distilling apparatus was solid, gleaming copper, and came to Aliceville by train all the way from Philadelphia. In Aliceville it was loaded into heavy freight wagons and dragged up Lynn's Mountain by straining teams of mules, over a road Amos Glass had built. When the size of his operation attracted

government attention — he did not even apply for the
necessary permits — Amos Glass raised and outfitted a
small army of hill men and would-be Confederates and
briefly blockaded Lynn's Mountain against an onslaught
of seventy-five federal marshals. For his efforts he spent
nine years in the penitentiary in Atlanta, and was saved
from a sentence of life imprisonment, or the gallows, by
his age and notoriety and the fact that no marshals had
been killed or wounded during their participation in
what he called in his final letter to the *Observer* the
"Invasion of the Sovereign Mountain by Republican Jin-
goes." The children of Aliceville were warned not to
speak to my father because he was Amos Glass's only
son, and therefore bound by blood to be the sole inher-
itor of the legendary Glass vanity and meanness. Strong
women blanched noticeably and looked the other way
whenever they passed him on Depot Street.

My father was four years old in 1905, when his
father declared war on the United States of America,
and thirteen when Amos Glass returned from prison. He
had been raised by his mother, the former Amanda Gentine, who was Amos Glass's third wife and, although
frail and prone to long sicknesses, a woman known
from one end of Lynn's Mountain to the other for her
great beauty. Both of Amos Glass's first two wives had
died young — one of tuberculosis and one of scarlet
fever — without leaving him children. My grandmother
was a devoutly religious, although understandably bitter, young woman whose father had given her in mar-

riage at age fifteen, against her will, to Amos Glass for a dowry of five hundred dollars and two and a half gallons of Cherry Bounce. Three times after their marriage she ran away and hid in the laurel high up on the side of the mountain, only to be hunted down and dragged back to Amos Glass's house by her brothers. She believed that the making or drinking of liquor of any type was an unforgivable sin against an Old Testament God, and she spent nine solitary years living hand-to-mouth in Amos Glass's big house, often on the charity of her family and neighbors, passing that belief along to her young son, Jim.

Amos Glass returned from Atlanta in the late summer of 1914 bent, at age seventy-five, on rebuilding his distillery and recovering his lost fortune and pride. He had been home less than a week when he dug up a small jar of money he had buried in a secret place on the mountain (to this day people wander through the laurel on Lynn's Mountain looking in vain for Amos Glass's legendary buried fortune; what they find are chiggers and yellow jackets and snakes) and bought a small still from Amanda's youngest brother, Robley Gentine, and began harvesting wild cherries for a new run of Cherry Bounce. My father, unknowingly beginning the legend of his life that would shape itself in my mother's mind into something resembling gospel, refused to help with the harvest. Amos Glass was haunted by the sight of the burned-out brick shell of his distillery, which sat directly across the road from his house, and he beat my father dazed and bloody with the limb of a wild cherry tree.

Over the next four years, Amos Glass regained very little of his lost fortune, and probably very little of his famous pride. His time in Atlanta had ruined his touch with copper and heat and mash. He regularly beat my father — and, angered by what he considered the betrayal that had taken place in his house during his absence, his wife as well — every time a run of Cherry Bounce turned dingy in its bottles, or when he drank moonshine with Amanda's father and brothers, or when the sight of trees growing inside his distillery and the thought of his age became too bitter to bear, until Amanda was bitten by a spider hidden in the kitchen wood box. Although the bite wasn't serious, Amanda Gentine Glass's heart stopped beating four days later. The day after his mother was buried, my father put his few belongings into a feed sack and left Lynn's Mountain forever. He walked to Aliceville, seventeen miles away — the first place he came to that could be considered a place — where he showed up at the McBride Feed Store one winter night at dusk and met Uncle Coran, who took him home to the middle house on Depot Street and introduced him to Uncle Zeno.

Jim Glass settled into the storeroom of the cotton gin and began eating regularly at the McBride family table. He attended the Aliceville First Baptist Church every Sunday from the time he got to town — although few people there spoke to him, and the deacons discussed denying him fellowship, and would have had not Uncle Zeno intervened and threatened to foreclose on the note he held for the church building — and sat with my uncles on their pew near the front of the church. At that time men and women still came in separate doors and sat on opposite sides of the sanctuary. My mother sat across the aisle from her brothers, with the other girls her age, all of whom, she often told me, sneaked looks at my father, because he was tall and handsome, but distant somehow, and had an uncommonly good tenor voice. "He looked just like you," Uncle Coran told me once when I asked, away from my mother, "so you know he wasn't that pretty." And perhaps because my three uncles were in fact talented singers themselves, and called themselves the Aliceville Baptist Trio and sang in revivals at churches in three counties and won blue ribbons at associational singing contests, they couldn't remember anything about the sound of my father's voice, one way or the other.

Jim Glass was not welcomed into the hearts of the people of Aliceville until six months after his arrival, when during the annual summer revival, after the visiting preacher's sermon about the return of the prodigal son, he went forward during the altar call and dropped to his knees in front of the congregation, and asked the minister to pray for the soul of his father, who was a sinner and did not know Jesus Christ. My mother said that the entire membership of the Aliceville First Baptist Church — including my uncles, who aside from their singing were usually nondemonstrative in their religious beliefs — then joined him at the altar and prayed as one body for the lost, black heart of the blockader Amos Glass. My mother often told me how she decided at that moment — as she knelt behind Jim Glass and stared at a single red ant slowly climbing the sole of one of his shoes — to marry the bootlegger's beautiful son. Uncle Al heard my mother tell the story about the ant on Jim Glass's shoe probably a hundred times over the years, but it meant something else to him entirely, and he never once told her about the ants that came for my father in the field. "What that ant on Jim Glass's shoe meant," Uncle Al told me in the hospital in 1974, "was that death was on him already."

My father was twenty-three years old when his heart gave out, ten years younger than his mother had been. My mother had just turned twenty in April, and had forty-six years left to live. I suppose that because she was so young, and my birth came so soon after my father's death, and because she did not see my father dead or attend his funeral (the last time she saw him, he kissed her on the cheek and walked away with a hoe over his shoulder), she convinced herself, or at least tried to for as long as she lived — by telling me the story over and over — that Jim Glass had died that day in the cotton field so that I might live. The whole time I was growing up, she never seemed to notice — and I watched her closely for a sign — that her story paralleled the ones from the gospel I heard in Sunday school. And because I was fearful of the implications of any scripture-like story in which I was a main character, as well as the sole beneficiary of grace, I pretended not to notice either. I sometimes saw my uncles shake their heads behind her back, but I never heard them contradict her.

My mother's story always began with my father walking into town at dusk and meeting Uncle Coran. That much never changed. But sometimes when she told it the sky was purple from the sunset and sometimes it was orange; sometimes there was no sunset at all, just the gradual quiet darkening of North Carolina in the winter; sometimes low, thick clouds moved in from South Carolina on a wind that smelled like snow. It was always cold the day Jim Glass came. Up on Lynn's Mountain, he and Robley Gentine dug Amanda's grave with an old ax and a sharp pick because the ground was frozen hard. My father and Amos Glass argued before he left the mountain, although, according to my mother, my father was a gentleman and never told her what they said. It took him all day to walk to Aliceville.

To this day Aliceville is a town that rises up for no apparent reason out of the farming country that surrounds it. When my father walked out of the cotton fields and into town, the first building he came to was the McBride Cotton Gin, and the second was the McBride Feed Store. There was a light burning inside the store and through the window my father saw Uncle Coran bent over the books, and maybe he saw the fire in the stove. If he turned around and looked before he knocked on the door, he could've seen the black hump of Lynn's Mountain in the distance, rising above the low hills he had just crossed. Uncle Coran said that it was just luck that Jim Glass showed up at the store when he did, and that the McBrides needed help at all. "If it hadn't been for the flu that year," Uncle Coran said, "I would've sent him on his way. And if I had ever been any good with the books, I would've been home already, where I should've been, and your daddy never would've found me." My mother, however, said that every bit of it was the will of God.

Like almost everything else about my father, the way he was dressed when he stepped into the light and introduced himself to Uncle Coran changed over time with my mother's telling and then gradually changed back. Although I do not know how conscious she was of it, my mother had a gift for knowing how to change a story inside its telling to make it more true. Sometimes my father didn't have on a coat, but sometimes he did; how he was dressed depended more on the climate in the room where his story was being told than it did on the weather the night he walked into town. The changes in the story came from what my mother sensed inside us as we listened. If my father wore a coat on his journey, it was always too small and his arms stuck out of the sleeves. His cheeks and ears were red from the cold, and he stood beside the stove in the store and rubbed his hands and held them out to the heat.

No photographs were ever made of my father — there were no photographers on Lynn's Mountain, and a Saturday trip on the local to the photographer's in New Carpenter always seemed to my parents like something there would be time for later — and partly for that reason I have always imagined, although I know it isn't true, that my father looked like Jesus Christ. The rest of it, I suppose, is Uncle Coran's fault. Uncle Coran and

Uncle Zeno took me coon hunting one winter night when I was seven or eight, and were sneaking drinks, of what Uncle Zeno said was cough medicine, out of stoppered bottles hidden in the pockets of their overall coats. We were waiting for the dogs to strike, but it was windy and dry that night and my uncles weren't optimistic about our chances. I stood with my back to the fire and my hands behind me and asked Uncle Coran to tell me about the night my father walked into the store. He glanced at Uncle Zeno and something passed between them and they both smiled without moving their faces. Uncle Coran scratched his head and said, "Now let me see. Zee, wasn't Jim Glass wearing sandals that night?" and Uncle Zeno snorted, once, and put his hand over his mouth and looked down into the fire, and did not look Uncle Coran straight in the face for the rest of the night.

At school later that winter I drew a picture of a man who looked like Jesus knocking on the door of Uncle Coran's store, with Uncle Coran inside working on the books. I told my teacher, Mrs. Weaver, that the man at the door was my father. She studied my face for a long time and went to her desk and came back with a rare gold star, which she pasted onto the sky above the McBride Feed Store. When my mother, who cried when I brought the picture home, showed it to my uncles that night at supper, they all somberly nodded and agreed that it was a very good picture, and worthy of a gold star, but were careful not to look at each other, or at me.

Later that evening, while they were in the barn feeding the animals, I caught them laughing and slapping each other on the back. Uncle Coran kept saying something I couldn't hear to Uncle Al and Uncle Zeno, and they threw handfuls of hay at him to make him quit. They tried to stop laughing when they saw me, and held their breath, their cheeks distended, until Uncle Zeno's escaped in a long, pig-like snort. Uncle Al pointed at Uncle Zeno and then grabbed himself to keep from wetting his overalls and collapsed onto the floor. Uncle Zeno and Uncle Coran ran across the barn and scooped me up and buried me in the hay pile. Uncle Coran had tears in his eyes. He carried me back to the house on his shoulders.

My parents began courting about a year and a half after my father came to town, probably before my father even needed to shave very often. My mother said that the day came when they both just simply knew, without even talking about it, that they were going together and would someday get married. That evening she set the table so that my father would sit beside her instead of in his usual place beside Uncle Coran. My father did not look at my mother that night, but did not complain, although my mother said that his neck was red all the way through the meal from my uncles' teasing, and that he did not eat much. Uncle Coran looked over the new seating arrangements and swore that the biscuit my mother had put on my father's plate was bigger than the one she had given to him, and demanded that my father trade. Later Uncle Al reached across the table with his fork and ate the food that my father left on his plate. Uncle Zeno belched ceremoniously.

Soon after, my parents began taking long buggy rides out into the country or down to the river, and sometimes did not get home until well after dark, which prompted the friends of my maternal grandmother to one at a time visit Uncle Zeno at the mill, or pull him to one side after church, and tell him that if he knew what was good for him, he had better keep an eye on what Amos Glass's son and his baby sister were up to in that buggy. My mother was sixteen. Uncle Zeno, who did not care much for anything done for the sake of appearance, and did not see anything wrong with Jim Glass taking buggy rides with his baby sister, told each of them in turn that he would worry about his business and family, and that they should worry about their own. Consequently, my mother said, there were some conspicuous absences at my parents' wedding, and that as a result, our relationships with some of the families in town were still cool, although she never told me which families. But on the red playground behind Aliceville School I formulated suspicions of my own and struck, as I imagined, blows that settled old scores.

On successive spring Saturdays before the wedding, in May 1921, Uncle Zeno took my mother all the way to Charlotte to buy a ready-made wedding dress — which was the talk and envy of all the girls in Aliceville — and my father to New Canaan to buy a navy blue suit and new black shoes. Uncle Coran loaned my father twenty-eight dollars to buy my mother a ring, and Uncle Al gave him a haircut. Uncle Zeno gave my mother away, and Uncle Al and Uncle Coran stood with my father. My uncles sang "Blest Be the Tie That Binds" during the ceremony while my mother avoided their eyes and my father studied his new shoes. Uncle Coran said that Uncle Al got so choked up during the second verse that he lost his note, an accusation that Uncle Al always denied. All three of my uncles were tenors, but managed to win ribbons as a trio because Uncle Coran, who always swore that in the first place he was a baritone, and not a tenor, sang bass in a falsetto voice and Uncle Al, who was the most talented singer of the three, sang alto. My mother said that the singing of her brothers on the day she married Jim Glass was the most beautiful thing she had ever heard. Uncle Zeno said that their singing was only passable at the wedding, and would not have won any ribbons.

For their honeymoon my parents took the local to New Carpenter, a limited to Marion, and a tourist excursion train behind an old, slow engine for the scary trip up Old Fort Mountain to Asheville. They stayed in a hotel with an elevator, rode the electric trolleys to the ends of all the lines, saw two silent movies, one of them a western, and savored the three meals a day they ate in restaurants and diners. They took a yellow taxi to the Grove Park Inn, but my father would not go inside because he had not worn his suit and was ashamed of his clothes. My mother went inside alone and later described to my father, and then to my uncles, and later still to me, the great stone fireplace in the lobby that would hold the trunks of whole trees. They made an appointment at a photographic studio on Wall Street, but the photographer stood them up. They climbed Beaucatcher Mountain late in the afternoon and sat on a rock and watched the sun set over the town, and made up stories about their old age and how their yard would be filled with grandchildren. They decided to name their first son James McBride Glass and call him Mac. They rented a buggy and drove to the gates of the Biltmore estate, and talked at some length with a caretaker about the rich people and marvels he had seen on the other side.

My mother and father came back to Aliceville after their three days in Asheville more deeply in love, according to my mother, than when they left. They settled down in the little tenant house on the outskirts of town, for which my uncles had stopped charging rent, and lived together for the remaining three years of my father's life. My mother still cooked three meals a day in Uncle Zeno's house for her brothers, except on Saturday night, when she made them fend for themselves and cooked instead in the little tenant house for herself and her new husband. Because Amanda Glass had been sickly and often bedridden while he was growing up, my father had learned to cook on Lynn's Mountain, and on Sunday afternoons, while my uncles and my mother sat together on Uncle Zeno's porch, and my uncles brandished tuning forks and hymnals and sang and accused each other of being sharp or flat, he often sneaked away to the tenant house and baked small lemon-flavored pound cakes or deep-dish apple pies for my mother, for which my uncles kidded him often, and without mercy.

During those days my uncles accepted Jim Glass as a brother, if they hadn't already, and began to work him into the family businesses as a partner. Their plan was for him to someday manage the cotton gin and one of the McBride farms. My mother selected a spot, just outside the town limits, away from the railroad tracks, for the house my uncles planned to build for them as a late wedding present. The spot she picked was right in the middle of one of the better McBride cotton fields, but on my mother's nineteenth birthday, my uncles met together behind the barn and agreed to give up the lot. It was on a slight knoll, facing the river on one side and the mountains in the distance on the other. My mother became pregnant shortly thereafter. My uncles threw their hats in the air when they heard, and chased my father down Depot Street and rubbed dirt on his face.

Although they were genuinely puzzled at first by the request, my uncles agreed to build a house for my mother and father that was different in design from their own. They were practical men who liked their houses — they were the largest in Aliceville — and figured they could do better and more quickly anything they had done more than once. But one Saturday my uncles closed down all the family businesses at dinnertime and went with my father in the truck to New Carpenter, where they walked up and down the streets until they picked out a house that my father said he thought he could live in and all three of my uncles liked well enough to build. They knocked on the door of the house and got the name of the carpenter. They visited the carpenter and after a short period of intense bargaining paid what they considered to be too much money for the plans. My mother, who was left at home and not consulted, locked herself in the tenant house and refused to open the door until Uncle Zeno promised to take her to New Carpenter on the local the following Saturday and show her the house. She pronounced it satisfactory. The house still stands on North Washington Street.

By the time my mother began to show, each of my uncles insisted on cleaning his own house and washing his own clothes. Uncle Coran and Uncle Al began locking their doors and hiding the key to keep my mother out. Uncle Zeno hid his dirty clothes in the barn, and Uncle Al stole them and put them in Uncle Coran's bed. My father assumed all the cooking duties, despite my mother's protests, and my uncles swore that it was an improvement. My mother continued to go to church, which at that time was considered an immodest act for a woman in her condition, and Uncle Zeno once again told my grandmother's friends to mind their own business. The family left the cotton-field lot unplanted in the spring of 1924, and scraped a road to it from the state highway, and on June 8, the day my father didn't come home for dinner, the lumber for my parents' house was stacked in the shed behind the cotton gin, and the corners for the foundation were staked out in the field.

Nobody cooked dinner that day — my father was supposed to — and my mother and my uncles poured molasses into their plates and ate it with the last of the biscuits my father had cooked for breakfast that morning. Uncle Coran made a joke about my father being asleep under a tree. Halfway through the meal, Uncle Al got up and put on his hat and left without saying anything to anybody. Uncle Zeno and Uncle Coran stayed in the kitchen past the time they usually went back to work, and tried without much success to convince my mother that everything was normal. They talked about working shorter days, or hiring more help, so that they would have more time to work on the cotton-field house. When Uncle Al did not come back, Uncle Coran nodded at Uncle Zeno and left as well. My mother talked to Uncle Zeno about ordering patterns to make baby clothes from the Sears catalog, and then put her head down on the table and did not talk at all. Uncle Zeno took his tuning fork out of the bib pocket of his overalls and tapped it against the table and held it to his ear and hummed hymns so softly my mother couldn't make them out. Fifteen minutes later Uncle Coran ran up on the back porch. He didn't come in, but stood to one side and motioned to Uncle Zeno through the window in the door. When I was a boy, my mother said that she knew right then, as surely as if a voice had told her, that my father was dead; by the time she told the story to my children, the voice had become real and spoke to her using her married name. Uncle Zeno slipped his tuning fork back into the pocket of his overalls and stood up.

My mother's story usually ended earlier, with my father walking off to the field with his hoe over his shoulder. My uncles as a rule did not like to talk about the days that followed, and most of the rest of what I know about that week, I learned from other people. The women who started for Uncle Zeno's when they saw Uncle Coran sprinting down Depot Street found my mother retching on the kitchen floor. By nightfall she had developed a fever; by morning she talked constantly to my father, and to her parents. She fell into a deep sleep around dinnertime, woke calm late in the afternoon, her fever gone, and asked to see Uncle Zeno. She agreed to stay home from the funeral only if he promised not to send anyone up Lynn's Mountain to tell Amos Glass, or any of the Gentines. She told Uncle Zeno that if Amos Glass came to the funeral, she would go there herself and spit in his face. Uncle Zeno agreed not to send word up the mountain, and wrote a letter instead, which he mailed to Amos Glass the day after the funeral. Uncle Coran and Uncle Al built my father's coffin out of wood they had intended to use to build a table for the dining room of my parents' house. My father was buried in the same suit and black shoes that he was married in. At his graveside, my uncles tried to sing "Rock of Ages," but could not get through the hymn, even though all three of them, including Uncle Coran, sang tenor. They started it several times. My mother lay in her bed in Uncle Zeno's house, freshly bathed and in a clean gown, already convinced that because her husband had died, the child she carried was destined to live a life that mattered.

When I was growing up, and my mother saw in me what she considered a lapse of character, no matter how small or temporary, she sat me down and told me that it was the Amos Glass in me trying to come out. If I made an A on a test at school, it was because I was supposed to make A's; but if I made a B, it was the Glass in my blood trying to turn me into a bootlegger. The letter B, for me, has always stood for bootlegger, and bootlegger, when I was a boy, was the thing I could feel every cell in my body straining to become, even before I knew what it meant. More times than I care to remember my mother told me after I committed some misdeed that Amos Glass's blood was the only kind of blood I had; I never said anything, but secretly thought that if I had more of Amos Glass's blood, and less of hers, I could have achieved some of the things she dreamed of. I have often thought about that day in 1905 when Amos Glass tried to lead a second secession, to preserve the brick and copper temple to himself he had constructed high up in the laurel. As he watched those seventy-five federal marshals march up Lynn's Mountain bent on preserving the Union he had challenged, on a road he had built, his small army of hill men dug in on the mountainside around him, when anything was still possible, I am sure he lived a kind of moment that I will never know.

What I did with my life was ride trains. I left my

mother and uncles and Aliceville and for thirty-seven years rode trains as fireman, engineer, and district supervisor for the Great Southeastern Railway. It is all I ever really wanted to do. When I was a boy, I watched from every classroom in Aliceville School as the freight from Elkhorn City took on water at the siding at the bottom of the hill for the last leg of its run to Hamlet. I was more interested by far in the black smoke chuffing from its engines, and from the engine of the narrow-gauge company train that puffed toward town from the cotton mills across the river in Roberta and Allendale to take on part of the coal that the big train carried, than I was in anything written on the blackboard or in the book on my desk. I suppose that I was no different in my love for trains than any other boy who grew up in a small town where steam engines stopped within sight of the school, but my complete willingness to settle for being ordinary, in my mother's eyes, was my greatest flaw. "There's too much Glass in you," she said when I told her that I had joined the GSR as a fireman. "And Glasses have no real ambitions beyond themselves. They do only that which makes them happy."

Over the years, my mother's story became harder and harder for her to reconcile with the facts of our lives. It did not make sense to her, or to anyone she told it to, that God would take her husband so that her son could grow up and spend his life riding trains. Nor did she approve of Christine, although I think that it had less to do with Christine Steppe than it did with the girls she had imagined for me. Christine was from Aliceville, and her dreams were no bigger than mine. When our daughters, Jennifer and Caroline, were born, my mother loved them well enough, but was disappointed both times that they were not boys. My uncles argued over the chance to spoil them, but my mother did not enter into the competition for their affection. Amanda Gentine Glass had lately become more prominent in her talk, and by the time it became apparent that the Glass line would end with me, my mother could not imagine a girl living a life whose story would have a suitable ending. My mother never completely gave up on me until near the very end, probably on the outside chance that even late I might still possibly do the one great deed that would make God's will manifest. Before she died, long after I had given up on her ever recognizing me again, she said, "Jimmy, you tell Robley Gentine I will pay him what I owe him, but he will have to wait a few days." And then she fell asleep. Later that night she opened her eyes and said with all contempt the last three words I ever heard her say: "You ride trains."

The McBrides have always chosen to be buried on their own land, and not shoulder to shoulder in a churchyard, among people who were not family. My maternal grandparents, W. T. and Colleen McBride, who died during the flu epidemic of 1918, are buried near the river, at the edge of a sandy field always particularly suited to sweet potatoes. They are buried alongside my great-grandparents, Mauney and Sallie

McBride, who picked the spot because it did not take up arable ground. My mother, however, chose to bury my father where he fell in the field, and not in the McBride graveyard by the river, and my uncles agreed to it, because they were McBrides, although when they plowed it would always mean breaking the rows on one side of my father's grave, and starting them again on the other.

Although many people in town considered the middle of a cotton field a strange place to bury a man, even one married to a McBride, my father's grave has always seemed as natural to me as a mountain in the distance. If you are from this part of North Carolina, the sight of the sky meeting flat ground will always make you lonesome. I can't imagine Aliceville without Lynn's Mountain rising above the hills to the north and west, any more than I can imagine the field where my father died without his tombstone rising above the rows. Whenever I worked that field as a young man and boy, I always looked forward to hoeing the four rows that were broken in the middle by my father's grave. I viewed it as a place of reward and renewal, not only for my father, but for me; it was a spot that by its nature forced me to end one thing, and momentarily step out of my way and consider, and then start something fresh on the other side; it made room inside those four rows of cotton, and the working days that held them, for a small, necessary type of hope. It is the same hope that I found riding trains and finishing a day of work in a place different

than where I started, the simple thing that in the absence
of a greater dream carried me to the end of my life.

The field where my father died and was buried came
to be known around Aliceville as the Jim Glass field —
all fields in the country sprout names, and all country
people know them — and in the years after my father's
death, I often saw my uncles' field hands take their
breaks sitting on the ground inside the iron fence that
surrounded his grave, rather than in the shade of the
trees at the far end of the bottom. That is something I
cannot explain, because there is nothing that a field
hand likes more than shade. Apparently, you do not
have to have a dose of strange McBride blood running
through your veins to take comfort at Jim Glass's grave,
although maybe it helps.

Many times I have sat with my back against my
father's tombstone, and looked down the long rows
toward the three houses on Depot Street, identical even
at a great distance, and felt his story buzzing in the air
around me, as indecipherable and many-tongued as the
voice of God. Uncle Al confided in me before he died
that he almost heard it too, the day he waited in the field
beside my father and looked into his eyes, and that the
words he sensed had somehow been on the tip of his
tongue, although he knew he would not have understood them, even if they had come out of his mouth. I
have come to think that maybe we are more than just
who we are inside ourselves, that we also inhabit the
stories that others tell about us, and that stories never

go away. My mother and all three of my uncles are buried with their stories in that field now, and their stories — the ones they told, and the ones they are in — add their words to my father's. It is hard to believe that Jim Glass has been dead for sixty-five years, and that we never met.

At least for the time being, there are only four tombstones in the Jim Glass field: the three that say McBride and mark the graves of my uncles and the one that says Glass, under which my parents are buried. And hidden inside those two names are the names Ledbetter and Lattimore, and Searcy and Hudgins, and Gentine and Womack, and Ruppe and Williams, and inside each of those names is a multitude of others, going back, farther than we can know, to the one original word. All names are words, and sacred in their way, and all words are connected by blood. I am not sure that I have lived a life that mattered, in the way that my mother wanted, but I have lived a life, and there is always something to be said about that. When my father's heart stops beating inside my chest, I will see in the sky the things he saw, and hear the stories he heard, before I go on to the thing that is next. We live in stories, and our stories go on, even when we are dead. If there is one thing I would like to say to my mother, it is that: do not worry, our stories go on.